Temptation's

Clutches

FOR LITERARY HEAT

www.BarbarianSpy.com

This book is copyright © habu 2015
habu asserts his right to be known as the author of this work.
Published by BarbarianSpy in 2015
Cover design © BarbarianSpy 2015
Cover image: manipulated: Copyright: PawelSierakowski
ISBN: 978-1-925190-51-9
All rights reserved

BarbarianSpy
Toronto
Australia

Temptation's Clutches

by

habu

CONTENTS

Chapter One

"Let's stop there. See, that place coming up. The one that looks like a castle."

Ron turned to Sally and gave her a look of disbelief—not to her face, because she was looking down the road toward where she was pointing.

"That place? You want me to stop there? It looks like—"

"I know, it's pretty much what it looks like—a glorified souvenir stand—but Susan told me we should stop on the way up. She told me it was a gas of a place to look through—junk like you wouldn't believe—a tourist stop in its own right. But it's also where Phil had that sexy photo of himself done for her. There's a photographer's studio there, and Susan says the guy there does custom costume photos."

"Yes, and it looks like there's a bit of everything else there too. Look at those lawn dwarfs and pink flamingoes," Ron said with a little laugh. But he slowed down and pulled off the road into the parking lot of an old Victorian house, including turreted tower, that had been stuccoed over and made into some semblance of a castle, complete with drawbridge and portcullis. At least it looked a bit like a castle if you stood a good bit off and squinted your eyes. A billboard sign off to the side identified it as Temptation Castle, home to the most exotic souvenirs and valuables in the whole Copper Lake region. "Look, is that a fitness gym advertised over the door of that wing over other? Talk about everything, including the kitchen sink."

Ron opened his car door and stood there in somewhat of a daze as his wife, Sally, and his two daughters bounded out of the car.

Sally turned half-way to the castle door and called out, "You coming or not?"

"In a minute. You go ahead," Ron answered. "I'm stiff from the drive. Got to do some unbending first. Maybe I should start with the gym."

It was a weak joke, but he felt a little weak. He hadn't been able to think of anything but the Temptation Castle for weeks—guilty thoughts, thoughts that surprised even him. He'd told himself he'd stop here on the way back to the city from dropping Sally and the girls off at the cabin at the lake. The one that the two sisters had decided to rent for the summer for the two families to share—and the husbands coming out for weekends. But he'd thought he was just fantasizing. He didn't think he'd really stop. And here Sally, of all people, had taken the decision out of his hands.

He knew far more than she did about what was to be found in the Temptation Castle—if his browsing of the Internet hadn't deceived him. Much more than he hoped Sally would ever know.

* * * *

It had all started when Sally and Susan got their heads together and decided they wanted to give the cousins a combined experience for the summer so that they wouldn't be strangers when they grew older. The sisters also both said they wanted to get out of the city. But they didn't want to go so far away that Ron and Susan's husband, Phil, couldn't join them on weekends and still cover their jobs in the city.

Ron and Phil had nothing in common other than being married to sisters. They were pretty much opposites. Ron was a chief financial officer for an advertising firm with a great reputation in the big city. He'd been grabbed up for the job because he'd been on a gold medal-winning Olympic rowing team and, helped by his clean-cut handsome athlete look, had done some national commercials for fitness products. But he also was very good at and conscientious about his job.

Phil, conversely, was a somewhat shady steamroller from the dark side of town, which had made him into an aggressive survivor. He owned a couple of nightclubs, and Ron was not just intimidated—and, admittedly also intrigued—by his gangsterish look and the size and physical power of him, but also by possibilities that sprang to mind of some of the seedier activities that made him successful with his clubs. Susan only talked about the jazz club and piano bar in the hotel. Ron wasn't even sure she knew about Phil's fleshier ventures.

The incongruity, though, was that Susan seemed to worship her husband and treated him as if he was a regular guy. They seemed to be a solid couple. And their two boys, in close approximation to the ages of Ron and Sally's two girls, were good, polite kids. The cousins got along famously, which was at the base of the pooled summer vacation plans. The sisters got along well too—it was just Ron and Phil who were slightly uncomfortable with each other. Ron got the impression that Phil looked down on him because he was so squeaky clean—he certainly found the club owner prone to just sit there and look at him with hooded eyes and the trace of a smirk on his face.

Ron had to hand it to Phil, though. He was the one who came up with the idea of Copper Lake and who wrangled the rental of a terrific house that gave each family a zone of privacy as well as common rooms where they could comfortably mix. And there was room to spare—they didn't even need to go up to the third floor with its one large bedroom with dormer windows.

Of them all, Ron had been the least enthused about this vacation arrangement. Ron wasn't sure how well he could mix with Phil, who intimidated him both for reasons he could clearly name and other, darker, temptation-related ones Ron couldn't manage to express. Phil had several times invited Ron to check out his seamier clubs, but Ron, though tempted, had thus far only been to the jazz club—and then as a foursome centered on the two sisters. Part of what made Ron uncomfortable with Phil was the looks he gave Ron when he made the invitation—like he knew Ron was tempted, and thus no better than he was.

As uncomfortable as proximity to his brother-in-law made Ron, the two of them would rarely be there together and the sisters and the kids bonded well. Some activities were shared, but the arrangement was loose and comfortable enough that each of the children could do his or her own thing as well.

Ron had wondered if there really were activities his daughters would enjoy, but it was Phil who had also settled that. He had pointed out to Ron that there was a regional Web site, where Ron could browse what was on offer—and Phil had given him the URL for that. As soon as Ron had seen that an introduction to camping was provided and that there was a horse stable for Cindy and an American Doll play club for Laurie, he was sold on the vacation arrangements.

It was on this Web site that Ron had stumbled on a link to the Web pages for Temptation Castle, and over several days, he had slowly been sucked into something he never in a million years thought he'd be tempted by again. He'd dabbled a bit in it in college—primarily in the form of watching and admiring the physiques of the other guys on rowing teams and comparing musculature and, eventually, endowments and getting a little glow off that. He'd even let a guy give him a hand job once, and had then thought, guiltily about that for several weeks. He didn't think it meant anything, though, and he'd forced himself to just not think of it again when he'd married and entered the corporate life.

The Temptation Castle Web site was bringing it all back and had done it so insidiously and slowly that he was deep into it—almost obsessed by it—now.

Temptation Castle was a collection of things. On the surface its main purpose seemed to be a store for novelty items and antiques and what it called "rare finds," which probably meant not-so-glorified junk and retail items no one had been able to sell out in the city stores and thus had consigned out to tourist traps like this one— although Copper Lake wasn't really a tourist trap sort of vacation area. This lack of competition was probably what kept it in business, Ron thought.

But Ron had already discovered that the Web site, which had a main page for the novelty shop and a couple of linked pages on other functions—the photography business and the fitness gym—and bio pages on the two men who owned the endeavor, had a deeper purpose.

One owner, a guy named Mart, who claimed to have had his start as a male model—and who looked Nordic in his photo—was the photographer and an artist too, Ron gathered. He'd done the art for the Web site, which used the shape of the Temptation Castle itself as a motif, although his rendering of it made it look much more like a castle than they'd been able to achieve with the real thing.

The other was a hulking, swarthy guy, named Theo, who claimed to have immigrated from Germany, and who ran the gym. Together they supervised the novelty shop.

What had led Ron down the garden path into the deeper depths of the Web site was the photography business. For Valentine's day the previous year, and while he was scouting out summer vacation areas, Phil said he had stopped at the Temptation Castle and had a sexy photograph made of himself for Susan. Glamour shots were all the rage then for women to have taken for their men, so Phil had one done, he said, almost tongue in cheek. Susan had loved it, though, and had run to Sally with it, who also loved it. Ron was a little nonplused. Phil was hunky, Ron acknowledged, at least to himself. He certainly worked his body well and had the body of a bodybuilder and the dark, curly-haired look of a man who was both trouble and sensual at once.

For the photo he'd been dressed in the metal-slabbed skirt of a Roman soldier that dipped down so low at the waist that the trail of curly black hair that ran down his sternum after flaring in from his muscled chest flared out again at the top of his groin and barely kept his manhood covered. He was wearing lace-up sandals and leather arm bands and was carrying a round shield held out from his body. The pose was provocative and left little to the imagination of the power and sensuality of the man—he had the musculature that seemed appropriate to a Roman warrior.

"God, that's beautiful," Sally had said. "So sexy. I want one too."

"You want an X-rated photo of Phil?" Ron had asked, the shock and hurt leaking from his voice—not because he didn't understand that she really wanted one of himself, but because he did understand and he was feeling unexplainable and conflicting violent emotions about.

"No, silly," Sally had said. "I'd like a photo like that of you. You're sexier than Phil is. Maybe a cowboy. I've always fantasized about being ridden by a sexy cowboy."

I did once myself, Ron had thought, but then he'd wanted to slap himself, and he'd changed the subject in embarrassment—the foundation of his emotional response to the suggestion was becoming clearer, and it wasn't something Ron wanted to admit to. That photo—and Sally—had germinated a seed in his mind. And the thought that Sally might think his body was sexier than Phil's aroused him, because he'd have to acknowledge, dipping back into thoughts he'd suppressed for years, that Phil's body was plenty sexy.

So, when Ron had clicked into the photographer, Mart's, page, he'd seen that he had links to galleries of his photographs. And the photographer had been really clever in setting the page up. The only gallery that would open up from Mart's page was gallery one, although there were tags for three galleries and something called "the chamber."

The photos in gallery one were totally innocuous—some artsy building and landscape shots and a few artistic ones of people—but devoid of sensuality. Well, not devoid altogether. The photographer seemed to have the concept of sensuality somewhere in the background of everything he shot—and all of his drawings, as well. This gallery included drawings as well as photos. And at the bottom right corner was a detailed drawing of the castle motif that had started on the main menu page.

None of the tags for the other two galleries and the chamber would open on this page, but they had subtle shadings of color filling in their backgrounds—green, blue, and red. And as Ron clicked on the tags without result after perusing the photographs and drawings on display on gallery page one and he became a bit frustrated, he noticed that small disks set in the castle motif drawing began to pulse. Three of them. Three different colors: green, blue, and red.

Ron clicked on the blue disk, but nothing happened. He clicked on the green disk, though, and gallery two, the one with the slight greenish tint to the tag background, opened up. These photos and drawings were more provocative. These were the custom-posed costume shots like the one Phil had had made. There were shots of both women and men—no landscapes or other themes now—and Ron found himself looking past the shots of women, which included ones in full French court dress, but with something extra about them—a reclining shot of the buttocks exposed or a frontal shot of an elaborate dress with the bodice open to the waist, nipples peaking out, almost but not quite covered by the spread bodice.

Ron had this bee in his bonnet that Sally had put there, though, and he found himself looking for the shots of men dressed as cowboys. They were there. Shirts full open or not there at all. Low-slung jeans with chaps exposing the jeans at the crotch, with a bulge or even the ability to trace the positioning of the cock. Expressions on the faces that showed either arousal or sexual satisfaction. Drawings every bit as revealing, with features even more accentuated than the real-life photos were able to show.

Ron found himself turned on and repelled at the same time, and he quickly backed out of the Web page and went off to another family activity where he could forget the titillation that these photos had brought out. He'd only gone this far because Sally had said she wanted such a costume-posed photo of him. He had thought about these things in college, when he was thrown together with well-muscled, nearly nude young men for long stretches of time, but he'd managed to put all of that behind him.

The next day, after the girls had gone to bed and Sally was cleaning up the kitchen, Ron slid into the den, turned the monitor screen away from the door, and opened Mart's pages at the Temptation Castle Web site again. He went through the sequence and clicked on the red blinking disk, deciding to go straight to the last gallery, but nothing happened. Almost despondently, he clicked on the green flashing disk.

Up popped a prompt. He'd have to register to see gallery three. In disgust, Ron clicked off and went to find a book on small sailboats. He'd sailed as a child, and having a big recreational lake outside the patio door of the Copper Lake cabin would give him a chance to renew the pleasure of being out on the water in a boat.

All day at work, though, Ron thought about that gallery three—and the one after it, the chamber. Embarrassingly, he went hard when he was thinking about those. And he felt himself trembling and the photos of men in gallery two swimming in front of his face. And the thought of him maybe being brave enough to have that photo made that Sally wanted and to have justification for being turned on by that too. They'd put it on her nightstand and he'd look at it while he was fucking her—and maybe she'd get an extra special thrill out of its effect on him as well.

Ron knew you could get a blind Internet account. There was no mystery to that. He'd get into the other galleries just by creating a cut-out account.

So, that night, when he could get to it—having thought about nothing else other than that all evening—Ron registered for gallery three—the blue one—with his fake e-mail address account and a plausible, but made up, street address, and he was in. He wasn't able to pick his own password; he was automatically assigned password TC46. When he saw what was in the gallery—which he assumed would be what was in the gallery—Ron almost clicked right back out, but something held him there. There were only three men featured in this gallery. Two of them were men who had costumed shots in gallery two— two particularly good-looking men, both of whom wore masks on their faces. The third one was Mart himself, in the Roman costume Phil had been photographed in. In a series of shots, the men slowly shed their costumes and ended up nude, laying on a bed, and holding an engorged cock.

Ron had trouble keeping his eyes off Mart. He was a Nordic god, big boned, and nicely muscled, and the primary muscle was thick and long.

Ron saw that each of the photo series ended in a video frame that invited him to click on them. Instead, with trembling fingers, Ron shut the Web page down.

A half hour later, though, he was back on the Internet. Getting access to where temptation was leading him on the Temptation Castle Web site frustrated him—he went back to the last pages he had viewed there and clicked on the buttons promising a video—but at each point he was asked for a subscription number before he could open the video.

Ron wasn't ready to commit on this Web site—to do anything traceable back to him. But he wanted to do something in his arousal and frustration—the temptation was just to great. So, using his fake e-mail ID and the PayPal account he'd opened, he searched for a male video site and joined and then started looking at the men who popped up on DVD covers. He was looking for a specific type—without even realizing he was. And, as luck would have it, he found what he was looking for—a blond Nordic god type—and pulled up the DVD. Lo and behold, however, he found even more than he thought he had been looking for. He found Mart himself, in the same setting Ron had seen on the Temptation Castle Web site—the Chamber. But it was a sequence that took the viewer beyond where Ron had been able to get on that Web site. Mart fucking another young man on the bed in the chamber—an example, no doubt of what Ron could see on the Temptation Castle Web site if he could get into just one more page in Mart's area.

Ron sat and watched the scene in horror and arousal, knowing he should turn it off but knowing he couldn't—knowing that this was exactly what he had been tempted to search for on this Web site.

The young man was lightly bound—his arms above his head, wrists tied off at the headboard. He was on his back, his legs spread, Mart's knees up under his buttocks, raising the young man's pelvis to give both Mart and the camera a good angle to watch Mart's cock plowing in and out of the young man's hole. Mart was working the young man's cock with one hand and his nipples with the other, and the young man was moaning deeply and writhing under Mart's expert spell. Ron watched the film through the ejaculation of the two actors and his own.

That night he fucked Sally like there was no tomorrow, and Sally got up early and fixed him a gourmet breakfast and cooed and made eyes at him from across the table as he ate it and coached the girls to wolf down their cereal so he could drop them off at school and day care on his way to work.

The next evening he watched all three videos and held his breath as each hunk masturbated to an arcing ejaculation. And each video ended with another naked man coming into view and sitting down on the bed beside the reclining first man. In two cases, it was Mart. In Mart's case, though, it was the swarthy and heavily muscled other owner, Theo. Ron was able to identify Theo, because both of the men had been in photos on the main Temptation Castle site. In all three cases, the videos ended there—at ejaculation from masturbation with another man sitting nearby. Ron didn't find this to be enough, however—not anymore. He went back to the DVD he had found of Mart's on the other Web site.

The next morning, Ron enjoyed yet another gourmet breakfast as Sally sat there in a loose robe with a sloppy grin on her face.

Now Ron was hooked. But now he was thoroughly stymied as well. He managed to get a page up by clicking on the red disk for the chamber, but it demanded not only his password but something called a "photo number." All Ron could think was that he probably would have to sit for a photo session to have access to the last photo gallery. He was becoming obsessed with seeing more action from Mart. Getting into that last page of Mart's was out of the question, of course, so he decided he'd just have to push that out of his mind. He found himself instead searching for another independent DVD of Mart in action at the Web site now subscribed to, but his search was fruitless.

It occurred to him then that he had just been playing with Mart's page, and Theo, the other owner, had been introduced in a gallery three video. Maybe the key to the red-lit gallery called the chamber was on Theo's Web page, Ron thought.

He clicked on Theo's page. He read Theo's bio with interest. It seemed that he'd been an Olympian as well—but Theo's Olympics had ended two games before Ron's had started. Theo's page said he'd been a heavy-weight wrestler for Eastern Germany. Theo's page was devoted to the gym housed in the wing off the castle. He had clickable tags as well and the castle drawing motif in the lower right corner. He was able to open the first tag, which was marked "Jousting Floor" and included photos of the gym and of men working out. They were all stripped down to athletic shorts, although if their activity required other safety equipment, they were wearing that as well. This page also used the blinking disks tucked into the castle logo, and Ron was only able to get as far as opening the second tag, marked as "The Lists," and he had to use his registration number, TC46, to open that one. It consisted of just a display of headshots and numbers. All of the numbers were like the one he was given, but they had an M appended to them. There were maybe fifty in all. They all were of men, some perhaps as old as sixty, but all well gymed.

To get any further into Theo's galleries, one marked as "The Dungeon" and the other as "Banquet Hall," not only was a password required but the ubiquitous "photo number" was requested for "The Dungeon" and a member number for the "Banquet Hall" as well.

Ron stopped digging further into the Web site at that point, but he had to admit to himself it was because the Web site had limited his access, not because he had the fortitude to just stop doing something that was both disturbing and dangerous to his lifestyle and the decisions he had made on what he would be in life.

Over the weeks before Ron drove his wife and daughters up to Copper Lake for the first time, though, rationalization set in. He found he was returning again and again to the pages that he could open from Mart's page and that he was increasingly letting himself savor what he saw. And, the biggest rationalization of all, the effect of what he saw—and what he imagined could be in that last gallery—had gotten him a lot of gourmet breakfasts and a fully satisfied wife. Sally liked to be well fucked, and Ron was now giving her as much of that as she could handle.

All the time he was driving Sally and the girls up to the lake, Ron was in inner turmoil. He'd stop at the Temptation Castle on the way back from dropping them off and maybe talk about having that photo made. The cowboy one. Sally clearly wanted one. But no, he couldn't do that. He was weak; the temptation was strong. It could lead to something else. The galleries were telling him that, if nothing else. But maybe that was something entirely different from having the photo made. Maybe those were other guys Mart had picked. Maybe Mart wouldn't be interested in doing that with Ron at all. But even though Mart's use of hired models was what Ron knew he should want—should take comfort in—it soured him to think of that possibility too. So, he'd just have to drop his wife and children off and go straight back to the city—maybe use another route altogether. Maybe not even come close to Temptation Castle again.

But now, here he stood, beside the open door to the car, watching Sally and the girls saunter into the jaws of Temptation Castle. Here because Sally had said she wanted to stop and explore the shop. The decision taken completely out of Ron's hands.

Now he could say that it was Sally who wanted them to stop here—and that he was only doing so to please his wife.

Chapter Two

"Wow, I think I've died and gone to heaven. Will you look at that, Ron? I didn't even know they made lava lamps anymore."

"With luck, they don't," Ron answered his wife, with a laugh. "Most of this stuff looks like it's been here forever and will remain here forevermore. Looks like their main product here is dust."

"And look, they have them in school colors. Do you think . . . ?"

"No, I don't think," Ron answered, this time with a snort. "Girls. No, don't run off like that."

"Oh let them go, Ron. What harm can they come to in here? Let's give them some space," Sally said. "They've spied Barbie heaven over there. They'll go home declaring that this is their favorite summer vacation ever, and we haven't even gotten to the cabin at the lake yet. Look up at the walls over there. There are samples of the photography. Not the sexy ones but glamour shots and in costume. Let's go over there and take a look."

Ron's family had scattered about in the cavernous shop room of Temptation Castle as soon as they had cleared through the entry gate, complete with drawbridge and portcullis that had been tacked onto the front of the building. Ron already had some idea why the girls shouldn't be left to roam in here—from what he'd seen on the Temptation Castle Web site. But he couldn't very well say anything to Sally about this. He'd just watch out for them in the corner of his eye. Meantime, he wanted to do some shopping and fantasizing of his own.

As advertised, the novelty shop seemed stuffed with every misbegotten fad item of the last fifty years. Both Sally and the girls were reacting like this was Disney World. Ron wasn't sure now whether they'd reach the cabin before dark. Good thing that Susan's family, coming from another direction, probably had already arrived, had taken possession of the place, and were setting everything up. Ron visualized Phil already in a bathing suit and sitting out on the deck, drinking martinis and supervising as Susan and the boys rushed around making the house theirs for the season.

As Ron sidestepped his way through the maze of overflowing shelves toward the left rear corner of the shopping floor, where he could see a wall of framed photographs and drawings hovering above a display of who knew what, his eyes were riveted on a large painting of a stylized castle set over an arched and stone-edged doorway closed off with scarlet red velvet curtains. It was the castle used in the motif logo of the enterprise's Web site. It was a black ink line drawing on an oversized canvas and was much more elaborate, all curlicues and hatch-mark shadings of detail that the size of the Web site versions didn't allow. There were circular swirls where Ron had seen circles on the Web site version, though, and they were tinted in the same colors Ron had already played with in the progression that had led him deeper into the Web site and a darker, building obsession that he was fighting—but without much success, and not enough will.

On this larger version, Ron could see letters and numbers on the circular areas that he was able to connect with what he'd played with on the Web pages. On the larger depiction, the floors of the castle, which was, Ron realized, an elaborate representation of the building they were in, were discernible and tinted. The middle floor had a slight yellow cast to it, and Ron could see a Y in a large curlicue to the right—and it even had "The Yard" written out in faint, elaborate script. Having seen that, Ron could make out other words now as well. The level above this one was tinted green from the left, fading into blue toward the right, and was titled "The Gallery." There Ron found three lettered and numbered circles, showing G1, G2, and G3, right where he had found the pulsing disks on Mart's Web page that took him progressively deeper into the maze, sensuality, and fetish of Mart's costume art photos.

Ron found that his eyes were searching for that last, elusive, area that had been called The Chamber on the Web page. And he found it at last, at the top of the tower—a C worked into the circling swirl near the top of the tower, which was tinted red, and the words "The Chamber."

Strangely satisfied and pleased that he'd found these markers, Ron let his eyes roam further—they went to the right, to the untinted wing, extending out in that direction, and he found a BH in a circular pattern and then the scripted words "Banquet Hall" nearly hidden in the seemingly free-flowing lines of the pen work.

His eyes went back to the castle proper and dropped to the gray-tinted base, where, after close scrutiny, he found a D worked into a circular pattern and then the words "The Dungeon."

Ron was trying to remember the logo used on the Web pages, wondering how much might have been discernible there that he just hadn't seen yet, when a mellow man's voice from very close at his side brought him out of his deep focus on the art work.

"Do you like it?"

Ron turned and almost blanched, as he was standing face to face with Mart himself. Ron's near-blanch rosied right up into a blush, with the realization that he'd seen Mart naked and in arousal already. It was a strange mix of feelings—embarrassment and an immediate sense of intimacy that Ron knew the other man couldn't possibly share—although the look he was giving Ron was level and appraising—and somehow knowing. Ron found his hands moving around his body, instinctively checking out that he, indeed, was fully clothed. And the man's eyes followed Ron's hands briefly before coming back and taking possession of Ron's eyes. And in that brief moment of diversion, Ron felt entirely naked before the other man.

"Yes," Ron responded in a voice suddenly and inexplicably thick. "Not my taste really, but intriguing. It's basically a rendering of this building, isn't it?"

"Yes it is. It's pretty much the logo of our little collection of enterprises here. Have you perhaps seen it before?"

"Ye—. No, no, of course not. But it's the sort of drawing that one thinks they may have seen before and that pulls you in to the details."

"Indubitably," the man said quietly. And the look he gave Ron conveyed that he thought Ron wasn't telling the truth—that he might have seen it before, that it was quite likely that Ron had been drawn to it because he had seen the motif before. And maybe more than seen it—that maybe he had already fiddled with unlocking its secrets.

Ron blushed again, something that people found surprising about Ron and that the man couldn't have missed. Ron was basically a redhead, although most couldn't tell that. The tones of his hair changed from a deep auburn with reddish-gold highlights on the top of his head down to a decidedly golden red in his pubic hair. So, when he blushed, he blushed rosy as any redhead would.

It often gave his emotions of embarrassment and befuddlement away, and Ron was afraid he was broadcasting this clearly to the man he already knew was Mart.

The man started to speak, but the tinkling voice tone of Ron's wife, Sally, broke into the moment. "Oh, look, Ron. Here's what I'd like. This one in the cowboy outfit, but more sexy—like Phil's—you've got a great body still. We need to capture that."

Ron broke eye contact with Mart, but not before he'd clearly seen the smile when Sally had mentioned his "great body," and he turned to his wife. "I don't know, Sally. I didn't think you really were serious."

"Yes, of course I am. It's just what I'd like to . . . oh, sorry." Sally had turned and seen the other man for the first time. It was her turn to blush and look disconcerted now.

"Ah, the glamour photos," the man said smoothly. "That's one of our little businesses here. Mine, actually. I'm the photographer. Are you interested in having one of those done?"

"No, I don't really think so," Ron said, but he was cut off by Sally's "Yes. My brother-in-law had a photo made here for his wife for Valentine's Day, and we've all been trying to convince my husband he should have one made too. My brother-in-law used that Roman soldier costume over there. But I think I'd like my husband as a cowboy—more sexy than this pose, though. I've always had a thing about cowboys. Don't you think my husband here would make a sexy cowboy?"

The man turned toward Ron and made like he was looking him up and down and, after giving Ron a "certain" smile, turned back to Sally and said, "Yes, I think he'd photograph quite well."

Both Sally and Ron were blushing, and Sally gushed, "Oh, I mean I know I'd like him to pose that way. Excuse me, I'm letting my enthusiasm get the best of me. My sister, Susan, and I have been joking about this so much that I couldn't wait 'til I could visit your store—this is a real treasure trove of a place. And I think my husband should do it. It would be great fun, don't you think? Phil's photo turned out so well."

"Your brother-in-law, Phil, was photoed in the Roman solider costume, you say?"

"Yes," Sally answered, "that's right."

Ron could tell from the expression on Mart's face that he knew exactly what Phil they were talking about.

"And your brother-in-law thought your husband would photograph well this way too?"

"Yes," Sally gushed, not having any idea the information she was conveying to the man that Ron knew she was—and his blush deepened as Mart smiled knowingly at him again.

"I know it's a little intimidating at first for many," Mart said, with a twinkle in his eye, "But they soon get into the spirit of it. I'm sure your husband would enjoy it. I know I'd enjoy photographing him." And then he turned and gave Ron another smile that assured him that he, indeed, would enjoy the activity and that he suspected Ron knew more about what that activity entailed than he was letting on.

"I don't know," Ron said. "Haven't thought about it. Maybe . . . maybe later in the summer. The family's up at the lake for the summer, so maybe later."

"Yes, I'd advise later too," the man said, moving his gaze around to take in Sally and the family's two girls, who were still dancing through the aisles and make squeals of delight at every new, fascinating find. "The process is a bit involved. It does take some time—and concentration. And perhaps you should come back for that alone, so we'd have time when you weren't worrying about your family getting bored."

Ron felt the tension flowing out of his body—and felt even more relief, cut with a twinge of disappointment maybe, when the man looked up, and seeing a clerk motioning at him from the front of the store where another customer was standing, excused himself and turned and walk away.

"Please do it," Sally whispered, putting her arm through Ron's and reaching up and giving him a peck on the cheek. "For me. You're so sexy."

Sally wasn't helping one bit, Ron thought miserably. As tempted as he naturally was, he was fighting hard against this—for Sally and the girls. And Sally was undermining his resolve. Although he felt his resolve quickly dissolving. "Yes, maybe I can find some time to come back alone," he said. "I suppose I'd have to have an appointment far in advance." He was still grasping at a way out.

"I'm sure I could accommodate you on short notice," Mart answered, the smile never leaving his face. "Here's my card. Call me whenever you're ready for it."

"Daddy, Mommy, come here quick," Cindy was crying out from across the store. "They gots Olympic stuff over here. Lots of it. Maybe there's stuff from Daddy's games."

Ron took the proffered card, and then turned and patted Sally's arm as Mart moved away from them. "Do you really need a photo to turn you on to me, Sally?"

"No, silly, of course not—especially not in the last couple of weeks. I thought you said it was too soon for another one, but . . . well, no I don't need the photo. But I want one and a photo would help keep the spark going for me. Please think about it. Maybe sometime this summer."

"Yeah, maybe," Ron answered. "But let's go see what the girls are up to now—and let's wave to Cindy to let her know we've seen her and are coming. I'm afraid she might pee in her pants from trying to get us to drag over there."

"This is Mr. Halterman," Cindy was gushing. "He says he put all of this stuff in the store—the stuff on the Olympics. And he says he was in the Olympics too—just like Daddy. So, you guys might know each other."

Mr. Halterman was smiling like he'd like to know Ron as they approached, and Ron was doing everything he could not be swallow his tongue from the realization that Mr. Halterman was Theo from the Web site and that Ron knew him a whole lot better and intimately than Mr. Halterman could imagine.

They shook hands, Theo almost crushing Ron's hand with the strength of his beefy hand, and Theo was saying, "Your little girl here—this is your daughter here, isn't it?—tells me you were in the Olympics too."

They shared identifications of Olympic years and venues and sports and realized that they had completely missed each other, none of their Olympic experiences having overlapped, but an Olympian was an Olympian, and there was an instant rapport establishing between them. Sally and the girls stood at the side, beaming, knowing how animated Ron got, how he glowed with pleasure and pride, whenever he met another Olympian.

Ron was surprised himself at his reaction to Theo. The man looked dangerous and menacing—reminding Ron of Phil—in the Web site photos, but there was an attraction there too—to both of them, Ron, had to admit. And the attraction to Theo was accentuated when meeting him in the flesh. Ron couldn't keep himself from grinning with pleasure at the meeting and trembling underneath like a racehorse when its trainer shows up and lays a hand on it.

Theo did have a hand on Ron's arm, and Ron was focused on that touch—a burning, firm-hold, possessive touch—while they reminisced about what little of the Olympic experience they could share.

"Most of this stuff is souvenirs left over from Lake Placid, to the north of our lake. I was there. That's what made me want to come back here to live," Theo was saying. "But I might have some from your two Olympics. You're welcome to sift through it to see if there's anything you want, and I'd give you a big discount on it. Maybe there's something from your year you regretted you didn't collect at the time."

"We'll see," Ron said. "We've been here longer than I figured. I need to get these ladies up to the lake. We're summering with my wife's sister's family, and they'll be wondering where we are."

"Maybe you'll come back later," Theo said. "If you get bored and your family is otherwise occupied, you could come down and use the gym if you like—for free, as my guest, one Olympian to another. I run the gym too." He was looking at Ron like he could eat him for dinner.

"Well, I don't know. Maybe . . ."

"You do work out still, don't you?" Theo asked. "You look like you do. Do you still row? Will we be seeing you out on the lake?"

"Not rowing, I don't think," Ron said, with a laugh. "I do hope to get in some sailing, though. I did that as a child."

"He runs now," Sally chipped in. "Real serious about it, too. He's run a couple of marathons and has done real well." Sally was letting the pride shine through in her voice. There was no question what she thought of her man.

"Runs?" Theo said. "Well, then, you'll want to come over here for the July 4th charity run we sponsor every year. Can I count on you for that?"

"Well . . . maybe," Ron answered. Normally he'd say yes in a flash, and Sally was giving him a frown, knowing he normally wouldn't be coy about such things. He'd have to walk around this carefully—he didn't want Sally to lock into the effect Theo was having on him. The date on the poster about the event the man was pointing to showed that it was on a Saturday, and Ron could certainly arrange to be here for it.

Ron wasn't reluctant because of the charity run itself. He was reluctant because of how arousing having Theo hold his arm firmly was—and the scene of Theo in the buff that kept flashing through Ron's mind—just the snatch of frames at the end of the video, where Theo, muscle bound and hirsute—and completely naked and in monstrous, almost animalistic arousal, sat down on the bed where Mart had just finished masturbating himself. Once again Sally unwittingly wasn't helping keep Ron on the straight and narrow one bit.

"We'll see," Ron said. "But now, girls, we've got to go. The boys will wonder if we're not showing, and we need to find the cabin before it gets dark."

Cindy saw something of interest at the other end of the aisle and pulled Sally away with her.

Turning to Ron, Theo said, in a low voice, "You really have kept your body in top shape. And brought back fond memories of Olympic Village. Do you know what my best memories were of Olympic Village?"

"No, what?" Ron asked, although the blush was starting, because of some of his own memories of the athletic dorms for the games.

"All those beautiful bodies, female and male alike." He was watching Ron closely.

"Ah, yes," Ron answered, the blush spreading enough that Theo couldn't help but notice it.

"I never fucked as well as in those two weeks," Theo said. Then he laughed, gave Ron a half punch in the bicep and moved away, leaving a beet-red Ron in his wake.

Neither have I, he thought. Neither have I. And the encounters and faces that drifted up into Ron's thoughts were those of other male athletes. Never before and certainly never since—but those were heady days, when all the hard-bodied young men and women felt invincible and on top of the world.

Theo moved to the front of the store, where he was leaning in close to Mart, and they were whispering.

As Ron and his family moved forward, Theo peeled off and Mart slowly crossed to intercept them at the door.

"Let your family go on ahead," he was saying as he intercepted Ron and took him by the hand, as if to give him a farewell handshake. "Let me tell you a bit about the photo procedure and cost—the photo your wife would like to have made."

Sally flashed Mart a smile, indicating her appreciation for having an ally in breaking down Ron's shy resolve, and she and the girls bustled out of the building and the girls crawled around on the statuary and bits and pieces of paraphernalia that lay about on the ground between the castle and the parking lot. Mart slowly walked Ron out of the door, still gripping his hand and with his other hand on the small of Ron's back.

"I'm Martin, called Mart by most," he said. "And my partner you just met is Theo." There was a pause; Ron knew Mart was trying to gauge whether Ron already knew this from having perused the Web site, but Ron did his best not to show that he did know. "We'd really like to you come again. And I do urge you to have that photo made. Your wife seems to really want it."

"I'm Ron," Ron answered. "And we'll just have to . . ."

"No number? I got the impression you already had a Temptation Castle number," Mart said in a low, husky voice. His eyes were boring into Ron's.

Ron blushed and then, with no intention of doing so, he blurted out, "TC46. Or that was the number given."

Mart smiled broadly. "Yes, I rather thought so—and hoped. If you come back for a photograph, there will be no charge for the photo shoot . . . because you already have a number and know what the photo shoot entails. And I think you'd really enjoy it. Oh, and before you leave, perhaps I should pin something down. It's the photos of men that drew you into the castle Web site, isn't it?"

In answer, Ron just blushed. But that's all he needed to do for Mart's purposes.

After Mart had backed away into the castle, Ron stood there, by the car, mortified and exhilarated all at once. But this was a familiar feeling for him over that last couple of weeks—ever since he'd first happened upon the Temptation Castle Web site.

* * * *

"Come on, throw on a swimsuit—or not—and pull up a beer. The wives and kids are out killing the groceries and we can have some mano-mano time."

Phil had been right where Ron had expected him to be when they had arrived at the "cabin," which turned out to be a seven-bedroom log home with soaring ceilings and stone fireplaces reaching up three flights toward the heavens and with great expanses of glass looking out on two sides onto the shimmering Copper Lake, named for the color that was evoked at sunset by the water's unique mineral mix.

Ron and his family had found Susan and the boys already boisterously exploring the cabin and grounds. The boys had managed to visit nearly every nook and cranny already, and Susan had just about finished a grocery list for the first week. Phil was on a chaise lounge on the expansive wood deck, stripped down to a skimpy Speedo and inhaling martinis. At least he gave the impression of inhaling them—there were two empty martini glasses and one half full one on the table next to him. He always insisted on a new glass with his new drink. He was ever watchful of his intake, as a man in the nightclub business had to be, so he insisted on being able to count the number of drinks he had, and he had the fortitude to cut himself off before he'd had too much to be able to function.

Ron felt tired and wrung out—emotionally as much as physically—after the long drive up from the city and the highly charged stop at Temptation Castle. He was both frightened and exhilarated at what he'd admitted to Mart—and what had been drawn out of him by both Mart and Theo. He hadn't allowed himself to think about his latent desires—what he'd given up in the search for a normal life, which, until he had started perusing the Temptation Castle Web site had been satisfying enough to have made the sacrifice. It was like a whole world that had lurked in the background but that he had kept closed off was bursting forth and there was little he could do about that.

Thus conflicted, had having suspicions on his brother-in-law's leaning, he'd just stripped off his Polo shirt and shoes and socks and stretched out on a chase lounge next to Phil's in his worn jeans, and accepted the cold can of beer Susan handed him. After a couple of swigs, he was close to dozing off, nursing a pleasant slight sexually arousing buzz. He had a hard on and was dying to finger it, but he was aware that he couldn't while lying here with the two families moving about. He tried not to keep the images of the naked Matt and Theo in his mind, but he was enjoying the buzz and thus didn't force them out.

As on earlier occasions, Ron had been both repelled and aroused by the sight of Phil's beefy, well-worked, swarthy, and hirsute body, and he tried to keep his eyes focused on the lake as he grew drowsy and they talked desultorily about the stop at Temptation Castle. Phil had reacted with pleasure when he heard they'd pulled in there on the way to the cabin, and Ron was barely awake when Phil was telling him that he was a member of the gym there and that maybe they'd break away when the women and children were otherwise occupied and Phil would take him there as his guest for a workout.

"Not needed, but thanks," Ron murmured. "Already have a standing invitation from Theo, the gym owner. Happy to meet another Olympian, he was."

"Ah, so you've already met Theo. Did he proposition you?"

Ron was too drowsy to answer, and there always was the chance that Phil knew this. It might have been this, the last comment Ron had heard before drifting off to sleep. Or it might have been the sight of Phil's near-naked body, one that closely matched Theo's, although not as overly accentuated with muscle as Theo's was, that made Ron dream what he did. Or it might have been a combination of that as well as the disturbing, enticing visit to Temptation Castle earlier in the day. Ron had never had a same-sex arousal dream before—or, to be more correct, he hadn't had them since leaving college and getting married and settling down in his cushy city job.

He was running through a forested area. The silence of the forest was uncanny and was made more pronounced by the sound of his own heavy, almost panicked, breathing. He was running fast and his heart was pounding, not from the effort of the running, but rather from the fear and anticipation of what was following him. The heavy breathing was in stereo. It wasn't all his. Someone—or something—was on his trail and was gaining fast. Ron wanted to escape, and yet he didn't. He anticipated something happening, something he was running from. But also something he was running to. Something he wanted to have happen even though he was doing all he could to escape it. Something he wanted with every fiber in his body, but something that he wanted to be inevitable, to be forced on him. Something that he could escape the guilt of wanting by running from it. He was running faster and faster, with some hope now of outdistancing whatever was following him. But with no hope of outdistancing it really, he knew. And in the knowing, he was exhilarated and excited.

The breathing in pursuit was heavier now, and Ron was slowing down, going in slow motion, the beating of his heart getting stronger, louder. A large tree had fallen across the path ahead. The yielding, fecund brown earth path wound in a spiral up to it, with a dense growth of spiky ferns on either side, phallic fronds winding out from the center of the ferns and reaching out, grabbing for his ankles, trying to slow him down.

Ron laid his hands on the log, ready to spring up with his legs and vault the log. But as he did so, a beefy, hairy limb was wrapped around his lower belly and he came down hard on his solar plexus on the surface of the log. The bark was rough and he'd landed hard, but although he felt the wind being expelled from his lungs, the blow was neither painful nor scratchy.

He rejoiced in the release, spared now any responsibility. Knowing what was coming and wanting it, ready to suspend all cares and guilt and obligations to anyone else.

He felt the power and silky hairiness of the heaving chest that came down on his back. He felt the beating of the creature's heart and heard its heavy breathing and the snuffling noise it was making. The pressure of the limb around his waist was released, and Ron looked up as two black, muscled, hairy arms reached up and black, leathery hands grabbed his wrists and held his arms out and above his head.

The slow, steady invasion of his channel came, as he knew it would, with fuzzy, echoing grunts and groaning noises muffled by the forest, Ron knowing some of the strained grunting was his own, as the beast's throbbing, hot poker—thicker than any normal poker—started to move up inside him.

Ron lifted his head in a silent howl of "Yes, god, yes!" Relieved and free at long last—surprised and yet always knowing that the satisfaction and arousal of the complete filling and possession would be like this.

The figure covering him close, holding him fast, rubbing a hairy chest against his back as his cock pumped Ron's ass materialized into the Romanian wrestler in the Olympic Village dorm who had overpowered and fucked Ron so gloriously in those hedonist weeks of his Olympics. In and out, in and out, ever deeper, ever more stretching. Ron won over, thrusting back to meet the virile Romanian's thrusts, moaning his want and surrender. Throbbing, throbbing, throbbing, two magnificent bodies moving in consort as a well-oiled machine. The sensation of ejaculating at the same time the Romanian did. Being handed over to the Romanian's teammate.

Ron woke with a start, jerking his hand away from who knows where, and turned his head, locking onto the eyes of his brother-in-law, Phil. Getting an inscrutable look from Phil. Five empty martini glasses on Phil's side table now and a slight chill in the air with the sun now dipping half below the branch lines of the pine trees on the far shore of the lake.

A sloppy grin on Phil's face. Ron suspecting where his hand had been before he jerked awake and not completely sure that Phil's expression could be wholly attributed to tacking too close to the edge of drunkenness.

He looked down and saw the wet spot on the crotch of his jeans. No doubt Phil had seen that too—and probably more.

Chapter Three

Ron roamed the big lake house while Sally and Susan bustled around in the kitchen. Wherever Phil was, Ron didn't want to be alone with him. Ron was embarrassed, wondering what Phil had seen and heard while Ron was having his wet dream out on the deck.

Whatever it might have been, Phil gave no indication he had seen anything incriminating. He appeared at dinner, dressed in expensive casual—much too dressed up for the lake—and announced that even though it was Saturday, he needed to return to the city that night. He said he'd stop at the gym on the way to get the workout he'd missed by coming up on Friday.

The women and children were so taken up with planning their initial activities that they hardly even heard Phil's plans. And for his part, Ron was greatly relieved. He would be returning to the city on Sunday afternoon himself, but he was just as happy that he didn't have to spend the evening assessing whatever look Phil gave him.

The wives had brought DVDs of requested movies still unseen, and as the families settled in front of the TV set in the great room overlooking the lake, Ron removed himself to the small den upstairs and connected his laptop to the Internet. He fooled around for some time, avoiding going to the Temptation Castle Web site, but he was only fooling himself, and that could go on for only so long. The only reason he was on the Internet was to tool through those galleries again and imagine himself stopping at Temptation Castle and going through the photo shoot process, rather than, as he intended, taking a different route back to the city on the morrow and avoiding temptation altogether.

As he looked through the galleries, he stopped kidding himself. He got up and went to the bathroom and returned with a wad of tissues, unzipped himself, and sat down at the machine. He scrolled to the video of Mart masturbating and joined in. By the time he was really keyed up, he switched to the DVD he'd found of Mart actually fucking a guy, and he watched that. Rod came at nearly the same time that Mart's partner came on the screen. Perhaps if he had not had that dream this afternoon, he might have denied himself this forbidden pleasure. But the dream had gone farther than either the video or the DVD did—he convinced himself he had felt the Romanian wrestler's cock inside him, even though he knew this really wasn't possible with dreams. But it was all becoming so real and tempting for Ron, and his resolve was beginning to dissolve. He certainly couldn't deny that that Romanian—and others on his team—had had his cock inside him for real.

Of course when Ron drove away from the lake house early the next afternoon, he didn't take the alternative route to the city. Of course he drove straight to Temptation Castle and parked in the lot behind the building, out of sight of the road, rather than in the front lot where they had parked the previous day. He told himself that he might not have done that if Sally hadn't bugged him again the previous night to have a sexy photo made for her. But he knew, really, that he would have stopped there anyway. It was good to have Sally to blame for all of this—but it was an empty excuse. He knew he'd be betraying his wife, and he knew she would recognize the difference between having a sexy photo shot and living a sex experience in the process.

Ron had pulled into a spot between two cars and gotten out before he stopped, in shock, and realized that he had parked next to Phil's car. If Phil had said he was stopping here last evening to go to the gym, why was his car still here on Sunday afternoon? Ron hastily got back in his car and parked it well away from Phil's Mercedes—where, he hoped, Phil wouldn't see it if he left before Ron did.

Although if Phil did see him, it would be Phil who should be embarrassed, not his brother-in-law, Ron thought. Phil knew Sally had bugged Ron to stop here for a photo session. Phil, however, had no plausible reason to be here—at least not today. He said he had to be down in the city working today.

For the first time Ron considered Susan's marriage to Phil. He had always thought Phil to be much too slick for Susan. The first plausible reason that popped into Ron's mind was that Phil had something on the side—and that she was up here at the lake. It had really been Phil's suggestion that had brought them to the lake for the summer. For some reason this possibility lifted a burden off Ron's shoulders. Phil no longer had a reason to look down his nose at his brother-in-law, Ron now felt. Now

Ron had something on Phil. Not that he could be sure, of course, and not that he could really do anything about it.

Ron no longer felt all that burdenless about it as he walked around the building and under the portcullis and into the great room of jumbled delights. Now he felt duty bound to do something about what he suspected—but who should he approach about it? Susan or Phil himself—or Sally? No matter what he did now, the situation would be sticky and he'd be right in the center of it.

"Hello. Ron, isn't it?"

Ron looked up and into the eyes of a smiling Mart.

"Have you come back for that photo session?"

"Yes . . . yes, I guess so," Ron murmured. "My wife won't let me alone about it. So, I might as well have a photo taken for her. But I guess I need to make an appointment to have it done. I didn't call ahead."

"That's quite all right. I can take care of you now. TC46. That's what you said your number was, didn't you?" Mart was smiling. He was having nothing to do with the "my wife's making me do it" lame excuse.

"Yes," Ron mumbled.

"I only ask because, as I said, it makes a difference in whether you have to pay for it. Depending on the photos taken, you may not have to. Well, come along; we can discuss that upstairs. Come through my red curtains back there. As you probably know, the studio is upstairs."

Mart had taken Ron with a firm grip on his arm and was leading him toward the back of the store, toward the large painting of the Temptation Castle motif. All innocence on the surface, but something more, much more, for those who knew the code of the colors and logos hidden in the curlicues of the intricate design—as Ron now knew.

If he was going to cut and run, it would be now—now, before he had walked through the red velvet curtains. Upstairs there would be opportunity to go only so far and no farther. But Ron had already been seduced well down the path of temptation. Ron knew he was going to the chamber in the tower—if that's where Mart wanted him to go.

Beyond the entrance covered by the red velvet curtains, there was a short, dimly lit hallway, then another corridor doorway, covered with a beaded curtain. When Ron pushed through the strings of beads, feeling he'd passed some point of no return, Matt touched his arm, turning him to the right, where a staircase led up, into the darkness.

* * * *

The first stop at the top of the stairs to the second floor was the costume room.

"Are you keeping with the cowboy motif your wife mentioned?" Mart asked.

"Yes, that's what my wife said she wanted," Ron answered in a subdued voice.

"OK, that would be that section over there. You'll need to strip all the way down and start back up with a thong—that is if your wife still wants a sexy photo. A thong. Tight jeans on top of that, as tight as you can take them and with the lowest rise. We'll want to see the tantalizing fringe of auburn hair down there. I trust it has the same reddish-gold highlights as your head hair?"

"Umm, no. I go more red the lower on my body. If that's a problem . . ." He was going red in his blush.

"No, certainly not. That should be great. So, lowest rise it is. Then chaps and a red checkered shirt, brown leather vest, red bandana around your neck, and a ten-gallon hat. Spurred boots, of course. Oh, and you can wear one of those face masks, if you'd be more comfortable. You can keep that on throughout the session, although it might defeat what your wife is looking for. I won't make you take that off—although I may suggest that you want to . . . later. And bring along a lasso when you come into the next room. I'll be in costume too. A Roman soldier, I think. Like in my video on the Web site. You saw that of course."

Ron, who had been rummaging through the pile of Western clothes, trying to remember what Mart told him to put on, looked up guiltily at Mart's question. A leading one to be sure. And when he looked up, he saw that Mart was already stripped completely down and leaning over a pile to pull out a metal-slatted Roman skirt. His buttocks were firm, globular, inviting.

"Umm, yes, I did. Yes," Ron mumbled.

Mart looked pleased, and he turned full frontal to Ron, giving him the full cock and balls look and scrutinizing him closely to gauge his reaction. Ron looked away and blushed even deeper. Damn, he thought. He wished he could control his blushing better. It was so revealing of his emotions.

He began stripping down himself, fully realizing that Mart was watching his every move.

"Nice, very nice," Ron heard Mart say when he was completely stripped. He looked up, self-conscious, surprised to see that Mart was still naked. Ron felt his cock going hard, no matter what he tried to do to keep calm and cool, and he turned away.

"Nice butt too," Mart remarked. "The photos will be terrific."

Ron was trembling, but Mart was humming.

When they were dressed, Mart invited Ron to go on through an open doorway to another room, which proved to be a photo studio. In one corner of the room was a stack of hay bales, one in front of a pile of three, and Mart told Ron to sit on the front bale. He then began to guide Ron through a series of poses, firing off camera clicks at a rate that was only economical in today's digital age, where unwanted shots could just be deleted.

Mart moved slowly in preparing Ron for the ultimate shots, slowly enough that Ron wasn't shocked by what he progressively was being asked to do.

The first step toward the sexy photos was having Ron unbutton his shirt and let it hang open, showing his fine chest development as he leaned back on the hay in a languid pose. The shirt came off completely from underneath the vest next, as Mart clicked away with the camera. Then the vest, leaving Ron's chest completely exposed. In some of the shots, Mart had Ron hold the lasso at his side.

Mart complimented Ron on the change in hair color tone from the fine down running across and under his pectorals, then down in a thin line descending from his sternum to his hard belly and flaring out again at the golden-red edging at the low-rise waist of the tight jeans.

After these last shots, Mart came over to Ron and let him go through the digital file of the photo shoot.

At this point, Mart asked Ron is he wanted to take the mask off briefly. "The sexy cowboy photo for your wife most likely will come from this set," Mart said. "And she'll probably want one without a mask. You can put it back on afterward, though, if you'd like to take the photo shoot to the next level."

Mart hummed and had Ron take a whole new series of sexy poses as they worked without the mask.

"These are good, but I would like to do even sexier shots, if you are willing," Mart said. "Then you can decide just how far you'd like to go for your wife. I've found it's always best to go a little farther than the subject thinks will be appropriate. You never know what the wife might want—and you are such a good model," he added. "I could tell you'd been an Olympian and have kept in top shape."

Ron looked through the digital images of the new photos. He knew he'd go farther. He knew he'd go all of the way if Mart took it slow. But some part of him was still reluctant, was telling him that this was wrong and that he was going down a very dangerous path and should rein in his desires and resist temptation.

"Yes, OK. We can go farther," he answered in a breathy voice.

Mart looked pleased. "Then let's move on to the next room, shall we? We have more appropriate backdrops there. You can put the mask back on now, if you'd really feel better wearing it."

Ron didn't do so, although he kept the mask with him—when they got to where he assumed this was heading, he knew he'd want to be wearing it. As ready as he was for action, he wasn't that ready to make it public.

The cowboy area of the next room was a section of wood rail fence in front of a sky-blue background with clouds.

"Take the jeans off now," Mart said when he had indicated the various poses he thought Ron should take on the rail fence for starters. "And put the chaps back on."

Ron was photographed sitting on the top rail of the fence with his legs spread and his feet planted on the lower rung. He was holding a long strand of wheat in his mouth and giving the camera the teasing and come-hither facial expressions Mart was coaching him into. Telling him how good his buns were, Mart coaxed Ron into turning to show them off for the camera as well.

It was here, in this room, that Ron noticed that Mart was beginning to shed bits of his costume as well.

Ron felt himself being aroused as he watched Mart prancing around in increasingly less costume. He mumbled his apologies at showing his arousal, and Mart told him in no uncertain terms that it was all part of the plan—that if Ron chose to move to the latter photos he would be expected to be in full arousal and that the photos would show this.

"We can go all the way with this, if you're willing. You've got a great body and a movie star face. We're already into the realm where you don't have to pay for any of this if you'll sign a release for me to exhibit the photos. You let me fuck you on camera and I'll be paying you."

This, of course, only increased the exhibition of Ron's arousal, and Mart smiled his pleasure at how the session was unfolding.

Ron blushed when Mart told him to lose the thong.

"Don't worry, though, we'll go slowly," Mart assured him. "The initial shots will be from the rear, showing those luscious butt cheeks of yours. Then that nice equipment of yours, moving from natural to hard. Unless, of course, you want to stop now."

"No, I guess not," Ron whispered, "although I think we're beyond getting shots that aren't hard," and he reached down and unhooked the thong and let it drop to the floor. Simultaneously, Mart dropped the Roman skirt he was wearing and he stood there, naked—and in magnificent arousal himself.

"We can always backtrack for shots—after, you know . . ." Mart said. "You'll go down again after you've been well satisfied."

Ron gasped and gulped in air, turned away from the camera, and leaned into the rail.

"Beautiful," Mart said. "Now look over your shoulder and given me a smile. Yes, gorgeous."

Mart hummed as he worked, taking shots from all angles.

"Three quarters front now, please, and hang the lasso on your cock."

"I don't . . . think . . . that will work," Ron muttered.

"Oh, I think it will. Look down at yourself. That hard of yours will hold up the lasso nicely. A full three quarters shot and a full frontal and then lose the lasso, please, and sit back on the fence and widen your stance and fondle it for me, please."

Ron felt himself blushing all over now.

"Terrific. You are a dynamite model. I don't know which shot you'll want for your wife, but you will definitely be a featured model on our Web site. You'll want to OK that if you want the password to the chamber. You'll want that, won't you?"

"Yes," Ron whispered—against his better judgment, but a screamed yes now. He had come too far not to want that.

"OK, we move to a whole new level now, if you are interested," Mart said. "You've viewed the galleries in the Web site, haven't you?"

"Yes," Ron answered.

"You know about the chamber then?"

"Yes," Ron answered. "Up to a point," he added.

"And you have decided to go up to that point?" Mart asked. He had drawn in close to Ron. Ron felt the tip of Mart's monstrous engorged cock on the side of his thigh and Mart's broad palm on the top of his thigh—both points of contact burning into Ron's brain. The first physical connection. Yet another point of no return. Ron searched his mind for any hint of rejection and pulling back. But he found none. He was breathing heavily.

"Yes," he whispered.

"You've been fucked by a man before, haven't you?"

"Yes," Ron answered in a weak voice. His memory raced back to the Romanian wrestling team at the Olympics. That hadn't been the only time, of course.

"A big-cocked man?"

"Yes."

"I'm so glad. You are so desirable," Mart whispered back. "And I have a big cock. Not all men can take it."

Ron shuddered, as Mart leaned in and took Ron's lips in his—but ever so briefly. He pulled back, smiling, and looking for some hint of reluctance. But Ron had none to give him. The seduction of Temptation Castle had worked its magic.

"Come then. Come through the beaded curtain. Come up the tower stairs to my chamber."

Ron paused to put the mask back on. He knew that from this point he would not want what he was preparing to do to be something that he'd want identified to himself.

Mart took Ron's hand, and Ron docilely shuffled behind Mart on numb feet as Mart led him over to a corner of the room and pushed aside yet another beaded curtain—another level of sloughing off inhibition. Here Mart stopped, turned Ron into him, took his lips in a deep kiss, and murmured, "You're going to let me fuck you, aren't you? If you go up these stairs with me, I'm going to fuck you—on camera."

"Yes," Ron whispered.

Matt then gently pulled him up a winding staircase into the tower and the chamber that Ron had seen in the videos on the Web site.

Before they entered the studio, Mart pointed to another door.

"There's a shower in there. Please—"

"I showered before I came."

"Please shower and clean yourself out. There are aids for that in the shower."

"Ah," Ron answered, his voice showing his embarrassment. What a novice he'll think I am, he thought.

A double bed jutted out into the center of the studio room space from a blank wall with a blue backdrop behind it. Across from the bed, nearly against the far wall, were three tripods, set at contrasting angles and heights. Each supported a fancy video camera. Stage lights were located along the walls on this side of the room at various heights.

"If you've seen the videos, you know what comes next," Mart said.

"Yes," Ron answered. He seemed incapable of doing anything more than forcing out an assent at every step.

Mart didn't seem to mind. As long as Ron kept saying yes, Mart seemed content.

"On the bed, then, please—and put the vest back on, please. You'll want to watch the screens on the wall behind me. I'll be running other videos above that—to keep you in the mood. And there will be music as well. Both are meant to help you. All you need do is lie back on the bed and slowly masturbate yourself to ejaculation. Take as much time as you can, please. If you find you have to come quickly, don't worry. We'll wait a bit and do it again and we can splice the tapes together. And see this signal I'm giving with my hand? Each time I give that signal, take something off—as sexily as possible, please. First the vest, then the chaps. The boots and the hat. Leave the bandana on your neck. And you can keep the mask on, if you want. If you don't, you certainly can take that off as well. You have a great, expressive face. We'd love to see that, if you are willing. I'll pay you $500 extra and give you an extra good fuck if you take the mask off."

Ron laid down on the bed and looked up at the screen, which began to run video of what he assumed he would find in that last chamber on the Web site that he now had gained the password for by giving Mart what he wanted in the photo shoot. Men fucking other men. On this bed. One of the screens showing Mart fucking a young black man and the other showing Mart's Olympian champion partner, Theo, fucking a barely legal young blond.

Ron had no trouble holding an erection and showing progressive arousal. The ever-quickening music helped, as did looking down from the screen occasionally and seeing Mart, in the flesh, working his own magnificent cock as he moved around checking what the video cameras were filming.

When Ron had ejaculated up his belly, Mart applauded and told him that he had done very well. Then he walked over and sat beside Ron on the bed. This was the point at which the videos went black in the galleries Ron had been able to access on the Web site before now.

But the videos he had just watched—so like the DVD he had found on the Internet—told him there was more—another level, a level his password would now give him access to from his own computer.

Mart leaned over and laid his hand on Ron's belly, and Ron felt his cock coming back to life again—already. He held his breath, wondering what came next. Knowing what came next. Having already made up his mind about that—at least a day earlier—even though he had tried to hide in self-denial.

"You saw the videos. You know what I have to offer to you now. Upon completion of this phase, you not only get access to the chamber on the Web site, but there are rooms on Theo's page that will be open to you as well. Very interesting rooms. Do you wish to proceed from here?"

"With you?" Ron whispered.

"Yes, with me."

Ron hesitated. "I want to, of course. I don't know, though. I've never . . . it will be painful. It's been several years. Maybe if the first time . . . not filmed."

53

"You haven't been fucked for a while?" Mart asked.

"Are those cameras still running?" Ron replied, suddenly aware of them.

"Yes, yes, of course. This will make this a favorite video, I think. You are telling me that you don't do this regularly—that you've been straight for several years?"

"Yes . . . not since before I was married. Back during my Olympics. I'm sorry, but . . ."

"A thousand dollars. On top of all of the privileges, we'll pay you a thousand dollars for getting you bent again on camera. With posting rights, of course."

Mart was running a hand between Ron's thighs, under his balls. A finger was at Ron's entrance and was thumbing it softly.

Ron moaned and he felt his pelvis lift of its own accord and Mart taking advantage of that to take fuller possession between Ron's thighs. Ron spread his thighs more and groaned at the index finger that had pushed a half inch into his channel.

"A thousand dollars if you let me fuck you rough—on camera," Mart repeated. "Fifteen hundred if you let me do it unsheathed. I can show you a certificate certifying me as clean. I'll assume you are. Fifteen hundred for bareback on camera. And not holding back on your verbal reactions to what is happening to you. I'll take it slow—until you adjusted to it—but then all out. Oh, and two thousand if you lose the mask. Your facile expressions are worth a million."

Ron moaned again, deeply. The index finger was more than an inch inside his channel now.

"If it's no, you'll have to say it's no. You'll have to tell me you don't want it." Mart took one of Ron's hands and moved it to his cock. "This is for you. You've seen the videos. This can be inside you. Deep inside you. You'll love it. You'll wonder why you've gone so long without it. You have a terrific body. Let me make love to you. Let me be the first in a long time. On camera. More than just experiencing it, you will be able to relive it—as a voyeur of your own first time after all these years. Total. Rough. Over and over again."

A second finger was at Ron's entrance. Mart had positioned Ron so that one of the cameras could zoom in on the invasion of his anus.

Ron looked down the line of his body at the cameras, drawn by a sound coming from there. Theo was there now, operating the cameras, moving from one to the other, zooming them in, centering them on the seduction. Theo was naked, and he was already hard—he appeared to be as large and thick as Mart was.

Ron's dream appeared before him. The thrashing in the woods, the hairy beast. The taking. He looked at Theo and knew that it had been Theo who had taken him in the woods in his dream before the Romanian materialized.

"The other guy, Theo. He's here too," Ron murmured.

"Yes, for what I'm offering Theo will fuck you too—on camera. Maybe we'll do you together."

Ron moaned, but he didn't demur.

"If it's no, you'll have to say so now," Mart whispered. "Otherwise, turn over on your belly, please."

Ron groaned, reached up and slipped his mask off, and turned on his belly. And then he moaned louder as he felt the wetness of Mart's tongue at his channel entrance.

"Up on your knees, please," Mart commanded. "Give me your ass." Ron complied, and Mart separated his butt cheeks with his hands, and moved his tongue deeper into the crevice.

It wasn't the money. Ron didn't need the money. It was the filming. He knew he wanted to see this. Over and over again.

He writhed and groaned and muttered to himself.

"Don't hold back. Be vocal. The cameras want to hear as well as see."

Theo had shouldered a camera and was waltzing around the pair on the bed now, taking close-ups, turning the volume up to capture every sigh and moan from Ron.

Mart turned Ron again and pulled him down to the edge of the bed. He lifted and spread one of Ron's legs and whispered to Ron to hold the other one out himself and then his fingers went to Ron's channel again, penetrating deeper now, Ron having begun to open to the attention there. Mart's mouth went to Ron's cock, and Ron gasped and groaned and murmured his pleasure while Mart gave him slow, languid head.

Ron was zoned out, concentrating on the music and the thrill of the moment when Mart rose up on his feet between his legs. Mart hadn't repeated the choices he had given, and Ron hadn't thought to address those either. And then it was too late. Ron cried out and lurched and arched his back in pain as Mart was entering him. Slowly but relentlessly. Inching in and holding while the channel adjusted to him. Flesh on flesh, flesh in channel. Plowing deeper and deeper. Ron was flailing about and crying out his undoing, all of which Theo was capturing on tape with a broad grin on his face.

Gasping at the girth of it. Panting hard. He couldn't take it; he knew it would split him asunder. And then he *was* taking it. And it was moving deeper inside him. Pulling out, to which he almost cried out his regret, but then in again, deeper. Ron groaned at the possession him. "Yes, yes, YES!" he screamed. Images of the Romanians fleeting in front of his face. Surely they were as big. But it didn't seem so now. "Oh, shit," he cried out, as the rhythm of pumping increased. "Oh fuck, oh shit. Oh, fuck me! FUCK ME!"

Panting heavily, Ron's hips beginning to move in rhythm to the slow pump Mart had started after bottoming out deep inside him. Mart's hand encasing Ron's cock, pumping that in the same rhythm, until Ron spouted his cum up his belly once more. Mart pumping on with his cock. Ron begging for mercy as Mart got rougher. Mart not giving him any. Ron moaning deeply. Begging now again for the fuck. Begging Mart never to stop, to speed up, to dig deeper. The look of surprise and shock on Ron's face, all captured on video, as he felt Mart stiffen and then jerk and then bathe Ron's insides with his cum.

Mart leaned over and kissed Ron full on the mouth. Pulling back and moving his lips to Ron's ear, he whispered. "That was great. You were terrific. I'm going to pull out of you now, and I want you to push down on your channel. We want a shot of my cum flowing back out of your channel. There will be no question of what we did."

Mart pulled out of Ron then and held both of his legs wide as Theo came in with the video camera and caught the stream of white semen Ron expelled from his channel.

Most of the lights went dim then. "The cameras are off now," Mart said. "We'll rest and then take another position. It will all be spliced together and make us both look like supermen."

"Again?" Ron mumbled in a faraway voice. "We'll do it again?"

"Yes, and again after that," Mart said. "It's always best from several angles."

Ron moaned, but he still didn't say no.

"Up on all fours," Mart said brightly when the lights flashed back on after they both had rested and Mart was able to go hard again. "I'm going to fuck you like a dog now. Lots of guys like that best."

And he did fuck Ron like a dog, Ron up on his hands and knees and Mart crouched over his hips and barebacking him once more.

"And now the style shot," Mart said in the third and last go. He went up on the bed on his knees, facing the cameras, and pulled Ron up into his lap, also facing the cameras. And Theo came in close for shots of both of their faces, Mart's chin on Ron's shoulder, catching the saddling of Ron, and then moving down the length of Ron's stretched out torso, lovingly following the change in hair coloring from golden-red-flecked auburn down to the golden red of his pubic hairs—catching Mart's pumping of Ron's cock with his hand and moving down to follow Mart's dick moving up and down in Ron's channel. Moving back to Ron's cock to catch his arching ejaculation toward the camera lens and then down again to capture the last jerky thrust of Mart's cock up into Ron's channel and the spilling of semen around Mart's slick cock as he pulled it slowly, and at great length, from inside Ron's channel. Mart releasing the arm hold he was embracing Ron with, holding him to his chest. And Ron falling forward, exhausted and moaning softly, onto the bed.

The final shot was of Mart, speaking for the camera, asking Ron again if that was his first fuck and when Ron murmured in the affirmative, Mart eliciting Ron's judgment that it was the most satisfying sexual encounter he had ever experienced.

"You will be on the Web site in the chamber room by tomorrow night," Mart told Ron when he'd hobbled to the door, long after closing time at the Temptation Castle now—except for the wing where the gym was, which showed lights blazing on both levels. Mart was doling out cash into Ron's hand. "That really was great," he said. "One of our best. Here's a card with the chamber password on it. You'll want to use it on Theo's page too. I think you'll be pleasantly surprised. And Theo didn't get a go at you. You'll be back for that, won't you?"

Ron groaned at the thought and didn't say yes or no, but all three of them knew it was a yes.

Ron shuffled painfully out into the night. Wondering as he rounded the side of the building whether it had been worth it. Agonizing over whether he had let temptation get away from him. But knowing, really, that it, indeed, had been worth it and that he wanted it again . . . and again. He couldn't wait until the next evening when he was alone in his city house and could see himself on tape—could relive what Mart had done with him up in the chamber.

The last thing he noticed as he was pulling out of the parking lot was that Phil's Mercedes no longer was there.

Chapter Four

Home in the city, alone, on Monday evening, Ron stripped down and got comfortable, with a towel, in front of his computer and opened up the Temptation Castle Web site. With trembling hands, he went to Mart's page and started to click through the videos of the masturbation scenes until he needed the password that Mart had given him, which opened "The Chamber" page to him. Checking the index and finding that there were many videos available, he scanned through until he found his number, TC46, and clicked on that. And there he was, stretched out on the bed, with Mart sitting beside him and fondling his cock. Then with a sigh and a gasp, Ron sat back and masturbated to the video of Mart fucking him three ways from Sunday.

Afterward he clicked back to the first chamber level and saw that they had posted his masturbation video there already too. He got up and went to the kitchen and took a beer from the refrigerator. He stood at the sink to drink it, gathering strength and stamina. And then he returned to the computer, thinking that this would be tamer than the fuck video so he'd just be able to watch it for curiosity sake. Even this video turned him on, though, and he found his hand going to his cock, and he masturbated a second time to the running of him doing the same thing on the bed in Temptation Castle.

When he finished, Ron was exhausted. He left the computer on, although he closed out the Temptation Castle Web site, suddenly beginning to feel defensive about what anyone else could track down on his computer use. He showered and laid down on the bed— his and Sally's bed—naked. He was exhausted, but he couldn't sleep. The images of what he saw on the Web site, matched with what he could remember of how he actually felt when he was doing it, had him so keyed up that he couldn't go to sleep.

At 7:00 a.m. he gave up and went to the kitchen, forcing himself to walk past the computer, and he fixed himself a hearty breakfast. He sat down at the table and found that his hands were shaking so bad that he had to hold the coffee cup with both of them. By 8:00 a.m. he had called the office and left a voice mail that he was sick and he was already back on the computer. He watched part of his own fuck video again, but then he switched back to the number index and randomly scanned through a couple of other sessions, staying with the ones that turned him on the most to the end and clicking out of the ones that were less appealing or he decided for some reason or another he wanted to go back to later, to savor more in the viewing.

By 1:00 p.m. he was bug-eyed and he couldn't pump himself to hard anymore. He stood and stumbled, first to the bathroom, where he urinated a gallon of piss, and then he lurched to the bed. This time he slept the sleep of the dead. When he woke up, it was getting dark outside. He was hungry and his cock felt sore from overuse. He went back out to the den and cursed himself when he saw the glow of the screen. He'd left the computer open to the Temptation Castle site, and the screen was pulsing, begging him to pick another video.

He couldn't do this again. He had to establish a routine of backing out of this each time he left the computer. What if he fell and broke his leg or had a concussion or something and the medics saw what he had been looking at on the computer when they came to get him. A nonsense scenario, he knew, but it was no worse than remembering what his mother said about wearing clean underwear whenever you left the house because you wouldn't want ambulance medics to see you with dirty ones.

It dawned on Ron as he sat down at the computer again, a microwaved slice of his wife's Lean Cuisine pizza in one hand, that he should be able to get farther into Theo's page now with his new password. He went straight to the bottom of the listing, to the one marked "Banquet Hall." He was frustrated to find that not only didn't it let him in with his password, but it also indicated that this section was subscription protected. The password did let him open the "Dungeon" section, however. Only a brief look there and he clicked back out in shock. He definitely wasn't ready for this now, if ever. The videos there featured Theo, in leather, in deep BDSM with a series of hot-looking men.

Ron went back to the chamber fuck videos. He was bleary eyed at 1:00 a.m. when he next looked at the clock, once again unable to bring himself back to hard. He turned off the computer at this point, showered again, and fell on the bed. He was able to drift off to an exhausted sleep fairly quickly.

He managed to make it to work the next day, but his mind kept drifting to the Temptation Castle videos, and his memory to what he had experienced in the chamber, and he'd go hard each time. He'd thought he would quickly become bored with the whole thing, but he was wrong. Each time he thought about it—which seemed to be twice every ten minutes all day at work— he'd go hard and would have to fight with himself not to move his hand to the sore bulge in his pants.

Each evening for the rest of the work week found Ron in front of the computer, finding new hot men being fucked by Mart. By Wednesday night, he found himself checking into Theo's "Dungeon" section again—and then, invariably clicking back out after only a few minutes of squinty-eyed checking. On Thursday night, he stuck with Theo's page through two videos and retired to his bedroom in disgust and pledged not to look in there again. He knew he was just kidding himself, though. He was already starting to find Theo's "Dungeon" scenes intriguing and hot and arousing. And his dreams that night placed him in bonds and positions that he would never have dreamed a week earlier that he'd be able to stomach, let alone moan for.

Determined to bring his new fetish under control, on Friday evening Ron left for Copper Lake directly from the office. He had spent the later hours of Thursday night moving around the house and making sure that nothing was amiss—that nothing would give away the autoerotic week he'd had there. The last thing he did was to erase the history on his computer. He had no idea if this was enough—but it was as much as he knew to do to try to cover his tracks.

Ron got to the Copper Lake house late that evening. The kids were already abed and asleep, worn out from a hiking trip up a nearby mountain. The door was also shut to Susan and Phil's bedroom immediately adjacent to his and Sally's. And Sally was waiting up for him, alerted about his anticipated arrival time by the cell phone call he'd made from a gas station down in the valley.

Sally was quite happy to see him, and she wanted to cuddle and fondle. Feeling guilty and not being able to tell her that he was well beyond being sexually wrung out from his week's session with the computer, Ron did what he could to accommodate her. But when they retired and Ron laid down on the bed while Sally was in the bathroom, he went out like a light. He'd told Sally he had a grueling week at the office, so she just let him sleep. However, she was awakened in the night with the wall bumping of the headboard on the other side of the wall they shared with Susan and Phil's bedroom and the sounds of Susan being fully satisfied. Sally reached over and started to fondle Ron's cock in a well-practiced routine of bringing him awake and to arousal, but neither worked. He didn't wake and she couldn't harden his cock. So, with a sigh, she turned on her side and tried to ignore the sounds coming from the other side of the wall.

On Saturday, the men went out on the sailboat Ron had rented for the summer. The boys had a ball, and instantly fell in with doing whatever Ron told them to do to keep the boat afloat and on tack. Phil, in his skimpy Speedo and with a thermos of martinis, sat back in the fantail of the boat and grinned lazily at Ron as his brother-in-law remembered the delights of sailing and moved here and there and everywhere, keeping everyone in the boat and explaining what and why to the eager younger members of the crew.

Ron almost was able to forget his new-found fetish. Almost, but not quite. With a pound of guilt, he found his eyes going to Phil now and again, noticing again what a good, firm body Phil had, and drifting off to fantasizing how he would look totally naked and in one of those chamber videos of Mart's.

Relief came right after dinner, when, as he had done the previous Saturday, Phil left for the city, claiming that he needed to put out a couple of fires at the nightclubs. Sally and Susan brought out the knitting and sat by the fireplace next to the game table, where the children played board games until Laurie got cranky and they all went to their rooms. While the two families were otherwise occupied, Ron, against every resolve he had made, crept into the upstairs den, fired up the Internet, and logged in the URL of the Temptation Castle Web site.

That night it was Susan who laid in her bed listening to the thump of the headboard in Sally and Ron's room against the shared wall and to the satisfied moans of her sister.

Looking for any excuse late Sunday afternoon, Ron remembered that although he'd gone through the photo shoot for the sexy cowboy photo Sally wanted, he hadn't actually picked one out. This wasn't something he very well could do over the telephone, so there was nothing to be done but to stop in at Temptation Castle, if only briefly, on his way back to the city.

Once again Ron saw that Phil's car was in the parking lot behind the building, and he parked his own well away from Phil's. Only then did Ron remember that he needed to either confront Phil about his philandering or figure out what his wife and her sister would want him to do about what he strongly suspected was going on.

Mart came up to him almost immediately upon his entry under the portcullis, all smiles and possessive touching. Ron looked around, embarrassed at what an unsuspecting customer might see and assume—and also on the lookout for Phil, in case he was there. But no one was paying them any attention, and Phil wasn't in evidence anywhere.

"You've come back," Mart said, sounding quite pleased.

"Yes, but only for a moment. I . . ."

"No regrets about your journey beyond the beaded curtain?"

Ron looked nonplussed, and then he remembered that Mart had separated the photo shoot and the physical sex at the beaded curtain guarding the door to the chamber tower.

"Uh, no . . . but I've come by just to . . ."

Mart had pulled in close. He placed his hand on Ron's bare belly, worked it up under the hem of his polo shirt, and whispered in his ear, "Have you seen it? Have you seen the video?"

"Yes," Ron answered weakly. The warm palm on his belly was driving him crazy, and he felt his cock stirring.

"That was really nice," Mart murmured. "One of the best. Have you seen the third floor? That's Theo's and my private quarters. We almost never take anyone there. But I'd like you to see it. To be with me. How long can you stay? Have you come to be with me again?"

"Yes . . . no. I don't know." Ron was struggling with himself. He had dared hope, but he hadn't realized he had until this moment. Still, some part of him had known—and hoped. He'd scheduled himself for tomorrow off at work. There'd been no reason to do that. He didn't have any plans in the city. Something inside him had told him that as nice as the session in the chamber had been, it hadn't been all night. He hadn't gotten full satisfaction.

* * * *

"Oh, yes, like that. Yessss!"

They were on silken sheets and a platform bed in the middle of an opulently furnished room. Ron was on his side, with his torso stretched back into Mart's, and he'd just come out of a long, sensuous kiss. Mart was stretched behind him, one arm wrapped under Ron's torso and a hand fondling and teasing one of Ron's nipples. Mart was holding one of Ron's legs up with his other hand. They were joined at the hips, Ron's pelvis rocking gently back and forth into Mart's groin, and Mart's cock buried deep inside Ron's channel, flesh on flesh, no barriers to channel walls undulating on throbbing, digging cock.

This was the third fucking in the night, each position new to Ron, each one moaningly arousing and giving Mart deep access in Ron's channel. Each one being recorded by whirring video cameras from three different angles.

The night was young, but Mart was masterful and virile, long lasting and quick to recharge.

They didn't speak for the next twenty minutes. The pace was quickening and Mart was concentrating on make love to every inch of Ron's channel. Ron moaned and groaned, holding nothing back under Mart's instruction to fully enjoy himself—to relax and give into it completely, there being no reason not to now that he was here.

Ron heard the whirring of the cameras and could pick out the reflection on the lenses discretely placed around the upper walls and in the ceiling. He knew they were being videoed even though Mart hadn't told him they would be. He didn't care. But that wasn't true. Ron cared very much. He couldn't wait to see the video.

Ron was on his back now, his thighs spread, his butt elevated by Mart's knees pushing under Ron's butt cheeks, raising Ron's channel to Mart's half buried cock. Ron's arms were raised over his head; he was gripping the brass rails of the headboard with white-knuckled fists, arching his back, feeling every inch of Mart as he pushed inside him.

"Have you ever done it bound?" Mart whispered?

"No," Ron answered, the word drawn out in a moan. His mind went immediately to the DVD he had found of Mart and another young man. Ron wanted it.

"Have you been to Theo's page?" Mart asked. He was leaning over, pulling black leather strappings from the folds of the sheets. Showing them to Ron.

"Yes, but just briefly," Ron answered in a hoarse whisper. It was true that he only stayed there briefly each time, but he, in fact, had gone there again and again, both frightened and mesmerized by what he saw.

"Why only briefly? Does it frighten you?" Mart was lightly running the leather straps along Ron's chest and flicking them against Ron's nipples. Ron groaned.

"Yes, it frightens me."

"But it arouses you too, doesn't it?"

"I don't know. I . . ." Ron wanted it. He couldn't deny that he wanted it.

"Yes it does, I can tell." Mart was flicking the leather strips against Ron's cock, and the cock was standing at attention.

"Yes," Ron whispered, "it does."

"And you want it."

A pause, but then, with a deep sigh, "Yes, I want it."

Mart leaned over Ron's torso without disengaging his cock and, taking one of Ron's wrists in his hands, strapped it to the headboard with leather strips. Ron didn't resist.

"The other one too?" Mart asked in a murmur.

"Yes. Please."

Ron was lifted to new heights of pleasure and arousal, all guilt dissolved with this symbolic, controlling restraint, as Mart grabbed his hips and started pulling him hard up and down on his cock.

"Theo is anxious for you to visit him too," Mart said as Ron began to writhe under him and moan more deeply. "Theo loved your video too—he said he wanted you that first time too. He could hardly restrain himself, but the agony of restraint is something that arouses him all the more. He wanted to make sure you were coming for the 4th of July charity run. He says he will give you extra attention." And then Mart leaned his lips to Ron's ear and whispered, "He's bigger than I am, you know. Huge." Ron shuddered.

"He wants to use you, to show you how much pleasure there can be in pain. He will beat you, and you will love it and beg for more. You will come for him like you've come for no one before."

Ron was too far gone in the fuck, ready to burst and ejaculate again, to answer. But there was no need to answer. The volume and intensity of his moans had noticeably increased. Ron's inhibitions and self-delusion were peeling away from him as he drifted ever closer to the center of the castle's temptation.

He didn't even realize until he had returned to the house in the city Monday afternoon that he still hadn't discussed with Mart which photograph he wanted for Sally. But this didn't upset him. This just meant another excuse for a trip to Temptation Castle—something he could lay at Sally's door. Or at least pretend that he could.

Chapter Five

"You've seen, haven't you?"

"What? Seen what?" Ron asked. He was skittish, both nervous and a little excited by having Theo stand this close to him. They were in running gear and milling around with the others near the starting line for the 4th of July charity race being sponsored by Temptation Castle. There seemed to be a lot of hunky guys around ready to race, patrons, Ron assumed, of the gym attached to Temptation Castle that Ron hadn't seen yet. Phil was there too, but he wasn't racing. A concession stand was going, manned by some of the guys at one of Phil's nightclubs, and he was walking around and making sure that was running smoothly—and looking over at Ron every once in a while. Sally and Susan and the girls weren't there. Phil had gotten them tickets to a new adventure movie premiering in a nearby town, and the women had agreed it would be boring just to be at the start or the finish of the race and only see a bit of it anyway.

Ron was a little disappointed that Sally had agreed to the movie so quickly—that his girls weren't there to cheer him on. Looking around, he thought maybe he had a chance of winning or placing in this race. Most of the other guys looked out of shape or too muscle bound for long-distance running. The women entrants looked like greater competition than the men did.

Theo, especially standing this close to him, was making the back of Ron's neck tingle. Theo was wearing running shorts and shoes, but no T-shirt. His musculature was magnificent, and the hair on his body gave him an aura of danger and a sense of the wild animal. A wolf. That's what Ron thought of—a wolf.

"You've seen the dungeon, the Web page, the videos, haven't you?" Theo asked. His voice was smooth, a little saucy.

"Yes," Ron murmured. "I have."

"And?"

"And what?"

"And what did you think? Something more? Something more than Mart has been giving you? Something I've wanted to give you from that first video session? Something I've been saving for you."

Ron began to question that and then shut his mouth again. But he knew. He'd been to see Mart twice since that first visit to the private quarters—and he'd finally ordered the photo for Sally. And he had it; he just hadn't given it to her yet. He didn't know now if he could have it on the nightstand, where she surely wanted to put it—maybe only bringing it out on special nights—on nights when she wanted to experience a special high when he was fucking her. He knew. He knew that Mart had videotaped the sex they were having in his third-floor bedroom. Ron wasn't stupid. He knew Theo would have seen those tapes. Not just the first session that he had filmed himself—but the later sessions where Ron had been less inhibited and had given his all.

"You picked out a photo for your wife. A good one. Revealing just enough. I would have picked out another one, though, something more . . . more . . . you know." Theo was standing very close, running his fingers up and down Ron's forearm.

Ron turned and looked toward where Phil was standing, guiltily turning his body so that Phil wouldn't see what Theo was doing. He couldn't tell if Phil was watching him or not.

"The videos in the dungeon. Did you like them? Did you like me in them?" Theo whispered. "Did you like the expression on the men's face—and how hard they got—when I worked them?"

Ron didn't answer, but he felt his body awakening, getting hard. Bondage and a bit of sadomasochism. Yes, Ron had seen those videos. He tried not to see them, to break away from them. But increasingly he was going back to them repeatedly, looking at them. Theo in each one of them—naked except for some leather trappings.

Ron's eyes went instinctively to Theo's basket in the vids. He was repelled at first, and then, slowly, became mesmerized while he'd watched the videos. Theo was huge and he had piercings. He had a heavy silver ring in his cock head and sliver beads running up the underside of his cock. At first in the videos, Ron had cringed and looked away when Theo was working the men he'd bound. But now, increasing now, Ron found himself looking for the scenes, studying those scenes. And he had masturbated to those scenes. He felt hopeless, sinking ever farther into the temptations thrown in his path.

Knowing Ron was involuntarily looking down at his basket, Theo lowered a hand and let it flutter over the bulge there.

"I want you, you know," Theo murmured. "I've been waiting, wanting you ever since Mart's first taking in the chamber. I've just been waiting until you were ready. Ready for what I have to give. I see you bound and helpless—experiencing all of the sensations I can give you—as I fuck you deep. I'm huge, you know. You've seen how big it is. I know you have."

Ron was shivering. He said nothing, and tried to look away. He could see now that Phil was watching him. He was panicked. Two different worlds. Ron had been trying to play in two different worlds. Could he keep them separate? Was there still any hope of that? He had already gone too far in one world, sucked in by temptation. The things Mart had done to him—and that he had enjoyed and begged for again. This was too far already. The dungeon. The level that Theo was talking about . . . offering. It was just too far. The fact that the vids were on the Internet—that he was on the Internet for everyone who could get into the Web site, not just him, could see— meant that he was way past his worlds being separate.

"You want me too, don't you?" Theo continued. "I waited until you did. You're ready for it; I can tell. Aren't you?"

"No," Ron whispered, the word coming out almost as a whine. Not sure he was believable even to himself.

"A choice. You have a choice in this race," Theo said. He acted like he hadn't even heard Ron's "no." "We will come to a fork in the middle of the forested portion of the race. You will have a choice then. If you go right, as the course is marked, you will be on the path to the finish line. If you go left you will be on the path to paradise. Do you understand?"

"No," Ron murmured.

"I think you do," Theo said. And then he gave a low, throaty laugh. "I will be taking the left fork. You will too, won't you?"

"No," Ron managed to get out, a little defiantly, raising his head and his eyes flashing at Theo now.

"Oh, I think you will. Will you be going back to your family tonight, or did you tell them you were returning to the city?"

Ron just looked at him, a mix of shock and defiance in his face.

"You were going to Mart tonight, weren't you? No need to deny it. He told me you were—unless I wanted you instead. Can you guess what I told him? There are deeper pleasures to be had at Temptation Castle. You know it. All night. I have delights to take you over the edge, again and again, all night. You've seen it in the videos. Remember, the left path."

Theo melted into the milling crowd. Ron was tense to the point of snapping as they lined up in jostling rows at the starting line. He shook his arms and hopped up and down, working at loosening the tension.

The starting gun went off and Ron took off like a shot, moving to the forefront of the pack. They ran for miles, up the mountain road, toward the lake. Ron sensed Theo close on his tail. He sped up, and Theo was still there; he slowed down, but Theo didn't pass him.

He could see the woods coming up, where the runners were to leave the road and run through the forest before returning to the road farther up the mountainside.

Ron got the impression that some of the runners were playing as teams, bunching up other players, using a few guys and letting others sprint ahead. These were some of the guys he had surmised were using the gym at Temptation Castle. It wasn't long, as they came closer to the path opening into the woods, before four of the guys were boxing Ron in and slowing down, not letting him break free of the pack.

But Ron also had Theo drumming in his brain. What Theo had said. What Ron saw on the dungeon videos. What Theo was doing on those videos. The wild, rough-taking animal aspect of Theo. Theo, pelted and animalistic, fucking bound guys on the videos; using devices on them and making them writhe and cry out for it. Theo's ringed and studded cock. The size of it. the thickness and length of it. Frightening and yet . . . and yet . . .

Ron was slowing of his own accord. The four who had boxed him in were ahead of him, and nearly all of the other runners were ahead of those four now. As Ron slowed down, one after the other of the stragglers were passing him. But not Theo. Theo was still behind him. Ron felt like Theo was hunting him, pacing him, waiting for him to tire.

Ron wasn't tiring really, but he was panting, breathing hard—and it wasn't all from the exertion of the run. It was from the knowledge that the decision was coming up. That there was a fork in the path head.

At the fork, Ron took the left path.

He was running through the forest. The silence of the forest was uncanny and made more pronounced by the sound of his own heavy, almost panicked breathing. He was running fast, and his heart was pounding, not from the effort of the running, but rather from the fear and anticipation of what was following him. The heavy breathing was in stereo. It wasn't all his. Someone— Theo—was on his trail and was gaining fast. Ron wanted to escape, and yet he didn't. He anticipated something happening, something he was running from. But also something he was running to. Something he wanted to have happen even though he was doing all he could to escape it. Something he wanted with every fiber in his body but something that he wanted to be inevitable, to be forced on him, something that he could escape the guilt of wanting by running from it. He was running faster and faster, with some hope now of outdistancing whatever was following him. But no hope really, he knew. And in the knowing, he was exhilarated and excited.

The breathing in pursuit was heavier now, and he was slowing down, going in slow motion, the beating of his heart getting stronger, louder. A tree had fallen across the path ahead. The yielding, fecund brown earth path wound in a spiral up to it, with a dense growth of spiky ferns on either side, phallic fronds winding out from the center of the ferns and reaching out, grabbing for his ankles, trying to slow him down.

Ron prepared to spring up with his legs and vault the log. But as he did so, a beefy, hairy arm was wrapped around his lower belly and he came down hard on his solar plexus on the surface of the log. The bark was rough and he'd landed hard, but although he felt the wind being expelled from his lungs, the blow was neither painful nor scratchy.

He rejoiced in the release, spared now from any responsibility, knowing what was coming and wanting it, ready to suspend all cares and guilt and obligations to anyone else.

He felt the power and silky hairiness of the chest as it came down on his back. He felt the beating of the man's heart and heard his heavy breathing and the snuffling noise he was making. The pressure of the arm around his waist was released, and Ron looked up as two muscled, hairy arms reached up and strong, hair-backed hands grabbed his wrists and held his arms out and above his head.

The wolf was at his door. Ron's athletic T and shorts had been ripped off his body, and he leaped for joy at the freeing action of that. He felt cold, hard metal at the rim of his entrance, Theo's cock ring. And then he cried out and tried to widen his leg stance as the beast entered him. Ron jerked as the metal ring rubbed across his prostate, and then he felt every stud on the underside of Theo's cock as it journeyed into his channel. Again and again and again. Ron whimpering, all of the fight draining out of him with each successive thrust of the cock. No fighting it now; the cock was working his channel hard. No going back. He was fucked.

He opened his mouth in a howl. "Oh shit yes! Fuck me! FUCK me!"

Ron lay there, panting and whimpering, while Theo pistoned him hard and deep, almost frantically in the first taking.

Theo held there after he'd ejaculated deep inside Ron, holding Ron still and in position until Theo's own ragged breath returned to normal. Exhausted, Ron was breathing in shallow gasps and whimpers.

The powerful Theo then lifted Ron off the log and threw him, belly down, over his shoulder and walked into the woods on the down-slope side. They hadn't gone more than thirty yards through the brush downhill when they came out into a parking lot that was deserted except for a small van with covered windows in the back and Temptation Castle painted on the door. Carrying Ron around to the back of the van and opening the two doors there, he lowered Ron on the floor on his back. The floor was padded with the foam used for thick exercise mats in gyms. Theo pushed Ron up into the van and then climbed in himself. He stretched Ron's arms out, with Ron watching him closely and panting hard, both fear and arousal in his eyes. Ron didn't struggle in any way as Theo cuffed his wrists to short chains hanging on either side of the back of the driver's and passenger seat.

He began to pant more heavily and moan more vocally, though, as Theo turned and shut the van doors and turning again, grabbed Ron's ankle and spread-eagled his legs, moved his pelvis between Ron's spread thighs, thrust his dick inside Ron's hole, and fucked him hard to completion for a second time. All the time, Theo stared down into Ron's face, grinning, and Ron tried to look away, but couldn't.

At the apex of the fuck, Theo stopped and held Ron still and grinned down at him.

"Tell me you want it," he growled.

Panting, Ron tried to move beneath Theo, tried to make him come. But Theo just laughed and held him fast.

"Tell me."

"It's too late, dammit. You already took it from me."

"I'll never complete you again, if you don't beg me for it now," Theo growled. "I don't want you to pretend this wasn't what you want. Tell me."

"Please!" Ron pleaded. "Fuck me. Finish me," he whimpered.

Another laugh and three deep pumps and Theo came in a flood.

Finished, Theo stretched out beside Ron and stroked his cock until Ron too had ejaculated. He then took up a leather hand whip with several thin leather strips and swished it around on Ron's chest and thighs and cock and balls, teasing here, flicking a stinging little bite there, while he kissed Ron on the lips and nibbled at his lips and ears and nipples, until, embarrassed, Ron ejaculated again at the new and titillating sensations.

"The Dungeon. Do you want the Dungeon now?" Theo murmured in Ron's ear.

"No . . . yes," Ron whispered.

Theo laughed and patted Ron on the belly and then unbound his wrists. "Not sure you would beg for it yet, though. I want you to beg for it. You'll find shorts and a T in the corner over there. I'll take you back to the castle, where you've parked your car. Go home. Think about it. Come to me when you will beg for it."

Ron was close to tears. It had been OK—barely OK—when he felt he had no choice. When he was being overpowered, crowded, allowed to feel that there was more than temptation, that all of the guilt would not be his. He recognized that this too was temptation. A higher level of temptation. He was being given the choice: move to a new plane in the temptation game or take the escape hatch.

They returned to the castle in silence, and Theo left Ron off next to his automobile without comment or even a look in his direction.

Ron was half way back to the city when he pulled over to the side of the road, trembling. After a few minutes, he turned the car around and drove back up into the mountains. Theo was standing at the door of the gym wing, a knowing smile on his face. He had changed into leather. Tight pants, boots, and a criss-cross of leather on his bare chest, meeting at a metal ring on his sternum. He was swishing a many-stranded black leather whip.

Throughout a night of passioned cryouts, belabored breathing, and deep moans and groans, Ron was introduced to the sling and bindings and whips and chains and ball weights and dildos and stringed ass balls and tit clamps and the electro glove—mild versions for now, Theo assured him. And, of course, he was mastered again and again by Theo's relentlessly hard and churning monster cock.

Near dawn, Ron was in the sling, wrists and ankles bound high on the chains, and Theo was standing between his legs, rocking gently back and forth, his cock inside Ron only to the point where his metal ring was rubbing back and forth on Ron's prostate. Ron was holding very, very still, as instructed, Theo was telling him the current operation was very delicate, Ron having every reason to believe this was true. Theo was inserting the third, progressively larger sounding wand in Ron's piss slit, slowly, delicately prodding the wand deeper into Ron's urethra.

Ron was totally exhausted, whimpering quietly, completely spent—except for that last weak burble of cum that Theo was coaxing to bubble up around the sides of the probing wand and dribble down the side of Ron's cock. Slowly extracting the wand, Theo leaned over and down onto Ron's chest and kissed him deeply as he slid his cock in to the hilt and his own flow bathed Ron's insides.

"That was the sampler," Theo whispered. "Will you be back?"

"No . . . maybe."

"Yes."

"Yes." Ron turned his head to the side and wept quietly. He was so weak. He was no match for temptation.

"Do you wish to go farther? Farther down the path of temptation?" Theo murmured.

"Farther?" Ron asked, in shock. "What's farther?" No, of course he would go farther. Each step he had already taken was too far. What was farther? What was really too far?

Ron hadn't asked the question verbally. Or at least he didn't think he had. But Theo responded as if he had.

"Ask Philip. Philip Galindo."

"Oh, god," Ron whimpered. Phil. His brother-in-law, Phil.

Chapter Six

"The Banquet Hall. Theo told me you'd ask about the Banquet Hall."

Phil was standing there in the foyer of the lake house, just in his skimpy Speedo, when Ron drove up late the following Friday afternoon, after a week of agonizing and self-flagellation—and, because of the temptation, hours on the Internet watching the video that had been shot of his session with Theo in the dungeon.

"The Banquet Hall. What banquet hall? And where are the women and children?" Ron knew exactly what Phil was talking about; he was just playing for time—fighting the temptation still.

"The Temptation Castle Web site," Phil said. "The last gallery on Theo's page. The one requiring a subscription. And the women and children are camping. They'll be gone all weekend. We have the house to ourselves all weekend."

"You know about that? The Web site?" Ron knew it was a stupid question. He'd known as soon as Theo told him to ask Phil about further temptations that Phil was in this up to his neck.

"Of course. This was my plan to begin with. Temptation Castle was there, of course. And I'm a full partner. Who do you think runs the club part? It's just another one of my clubs. Mart runs the store and photography studio, Theo the gym—and I run the men's club that's fronted by the gym."

"The club part?"

"We'll come to that. This whole summer thing is because I want to fuck you, and I wanted you ready to want it too. The lake vacation, the house, all my idea. I made no secret of that. And if you were perceptive, you'd know I want you."

Ron was perceptive enough; he'd just been in denial about that.

"I've known every step you've taken into temptation, Ron. You know, you must have really wanted this, because you didn't struggle very hard. It helped for me to get Susan to have Sally pester you about that sexy photo shot. But you sank so fast into the temptation of the castle that Mart and Theo had a little trouble staying ahead of you."

Ron didn't answer. He just looked down at the floor. He couldn't dispute that. Temptation had been there, but he had done little to fight it. And he was ashamed to admit it—but he didn't regret having fallen to it. Even knowing what was happening now, he couldn't say that he didn't want it. He was relieved, in fact, now that it was in the open and now that Phil was taking the initiative. And suddenly all inhibitions of recognizing that Phil aroused him were cleared away.

"Come down to the lake. We're going for a swim."

"A swim? It's nearly dark."

"I don't care. A swim and then I'll tell you about the banquet hall. I'll show you the banquet hall."

Ron stood there, between temptation and common sense.

Phil fucked Ron in the water, under the pier. Ron knew why they were going swimming. Phil dove in off the pier and then, a few minutes later, Ron, still struggling with himself, but the temptation too great, dove in as well. Phil was already hard. So was Ron, conditioned for weeks to fall to this temptation. Phil pushed Ron up against a pier, under the dock, standing in water up to their nipples. They kissed as Phil stripped both swimsuits off and lifted Ron in the water, with palms on butt cheeks, and setting his now well-reamed and quickly opening channel on his cock head. Ron grunted and groaned as his channel descended on Phil's skewering cock.

Ron sighed and hooked his legs on Phil's hips and closed his eyes, shutting the whole world out other than the focus of the cock churning in his channel, as Phil rubbed his back up and down on the slimy wall of the pier in the raising and lowering of Ron's channel on his cock.

They came almost simultaneously in a shared, long sigh of satisfaction.

"I wanted to have you before showing you the banquet hall," Phil whispered in Ron's ear. "It was so long in the making. But it was worth it. And of course now I'll have you again and again."

"I don't understand; showing me the banquet hall?" Ron answered.

"Come up to the house," Phil said. "Use a towel. Dry off. But come up to the house. Don't bother to dress."

Phil was silent, not responding to any of Ron's questions as they came out of the lake, dried off with the towels they'd brought down to the lake, and padded, naked, up to the house, which was ablaze with lights, just as Ron had found it when he arrived.

"To the den, where the computer is," Phil said. They went in there. The computer was already on, and the Temptation Castle Web site home page was humming along. Phil sat Ron down at the computer and clicked into Theo's page and then on to the page that had been tagged "The Lists," the one with the rows of head shots of men.

"You didn't take a very good look at this ever, did you?" Phil asked. "You could get this far with just the password, but you didn't look at the photos, did you?"

"No, not much," Ron answered. Of course he hadn't looked at head shoots, not when all of those explicit videos were to be had. He hadn't had the time or energy to look at them.

"Because if you had looked at them, you would have seen my photo right there," Phil said. Ron looked at where Phil's index finger was touching the computer screen, and, sure enough, Phil's photo was there.

"Now for the banquet hall," Phil said. He leaned over Ron's body and tapped in a password, and the banquet hall page opened. Video after video of a rolling orgy, a swirling mass of men fucking men, all together, and many on one, and even men's asses being taken by two other men at once.

Ron didn't want to look, but it was fascinating, and so he became absorbed in what he was seeing.

"It's a men's club," Phil whispered in his ear before taking the lobe between his teeth and applying pressure. "The members of the gym are eligible to be members of the club, if they can afford it. I'll be happy to waive your fee—family rates and all that. They can come and exercise—on the first floor of the gym wing. And when they want they can go up to the second floor and play in the pile. And they can even go to Theo's dungeon, as it pleases them. I'm sure you will be going there."

Ron turned and looked at Phil, the shock showing in his face.

"Yes, I've seen the video of you with Theo in the dungeon already," Phil said. "Theo couldn't wait to show it to me. You've been a busy little boy."

Phil was leaning over Ron from the back and running a hand down to Ron's dick and encircling it and stroking it. Ron sighed and turned his face to his brother-in-law and they kissed deeply. But not for long; Ron wanted to open another video.

"I manage the club," Phil said. "Own it really, as my share of the operation. After tonight you'll be one of us, a member. You will then have experienced the full range of temptations the castle has to offer."

Ron was barely listening to Phil. His eyes and attention were glued to the orgies unfolding before him. He winced at the double takings, but he didn't take his eyes away from them. He could almost feel himself moving deeper into the levels of temptation.

"Do you see that?" Phil whispered in Ron's ear. That's Doug and that's Max. The guy between them, that's Spencer. Look at the expression on his face. Look at him struggle between them, as they face each other, sharing his channel.

"Oh, god, oh god," Ron murmured. "I didn't even know . . ." He couldn't go on. He watched, eyes locked onto the scene being played out, his hips in slow, rolling movement. Phil opened the hand encircling Ron's cock as, without even being aware of it, intent on watching the two men working the third between them, Ron's cock slid up and down against Phil's palm.

When Ron ejaculated into Phil's hand, he was as much surprised that he had, as wondering—and still a bit disturbed—that he was so easily tempted.

"Come. Come to the bedroom at the top of the house. The one we don't use; the one that neither Sally nor Susan has a reason to go to." Phil was saying it in sugared tones, but there was little question that he was to be obeyed.

Ron didn't mind that he would enjoy another fucking from Phil—especially now when all of the questioning and doubt were gone. Phil would take care of everything. He'd see to it that neither of the women or their children would know. It would just be something he and Phil did without them being aware of it. The families came together often. There always were opportunities. Why, even tonight, the women and children weren't here. They were off camping. That certainly was fortuitous.

Ron stood and padded out of the den and up the stairs to the third floor, the large dormer bedroom at the top of the house, following Phil. Even here Phil had been sensitive and had thought this out. No guilt of them fucking in any of the beds the rest of the family was using.

They reached the top of the stairs, and Phil turned and grabbed onto Ron's forearm and whipped him into the room—into the middle of the room, where he bumped into and fell on the bed that had been pulled out into the middle of the chamber. Flood lights clicked on, video cameras started rolling, and a dozen naked men reached out, grabbing for Ron.

Phil turned and padded back down the stairs, stopping half way and sitting down on the stairs to enjoy the sounds of Ron's surprised pleadings and moans and groans. He was gurgling now. Phil was almost sorry he wasn't in the room—to watch. But he'd let the boys have their evening. And there would always be the video. Then Ron would have seen, felt, experienced it all. And afterward Phil would take him and bathe him and comfort him and have Ron all to himself.

Phil picked out the voices arching out over the others. Doug and Max. And Ron's high-pitched wail . . . and his scream . . . and Doug's and Max's laughter and cries of shared passion. Phil lowered his hand to his cock, stroking himself, joining with Doug and Max in Ron's succumbing to the ultimate temptation.

* * * *

The transfer to Los Angeles—to Hollywood really—where Ron's advertising firm thought they could put Ron's experience and talents with commercial design and modeling to better use than on the East Coast came at the end of a momentous summer. First had been the blowup in Susan and Phil's marriage when Susan had gotten around to visiting one of Phil's clubs in Trenton, New Jersey, only to find that it was a gay strip club. She'd nosed around there long enough to discover that Phil was a "hands-on" manager. From that point, she had dug deeper and uncovered so much about Phil's interests—both professional and personal—that she pulled the plug on him, uprooted their boys, and retreated clear across the continent, to San Diego, where her and Sally's family was from.

This fast and total turn of events scared the shit out of Ron. He realized that it so easily could happen to him as well—and just as fast and totally as it had to Phil.

Beyond that Ron was afraid that Phil would spill the beans about him in revenge, but as far as he could determine, he hadn't done so. With luck Phil had been too taken up with the struggle with Susan and the attempt to contain the damage to get around to spreading the revenge out. And now it was too late. Late in the summer, lightning had struck Temptation Castle—literally—and the old wooden structure, packed with flammables, had gone up like a lit matchbox. Phil had perished in the fire. Ron had no idea whether Matt and Theo had as well, and he wasn't about to worry that scab. It had been all he could do to start distancing himself from that whole, dangerous world as the fantasy of the experience began to wear down to the danger of it.

As an Olympic athlete once, he'd had to discipline himself hard and to deny himself many pleasures that didn't contribute to his athletic success. As the summer wore on, with his young daughters out of school, Ron had more than enough time to appreciate how important his family was to him. So, he'd gone cold turkey on the male-male sex—even before Susan and Phil had split and Phil had gone up in flames. He'd done it before. Now, when the stakes were even higher, he was determined to do it again. By the time temptation had blazed up and been reduced to ashes, Ron and his family were in Los Angeles. The offer on the California transfer had come up several times in the previous two years. It took Susan taking her family west to cause Sally to want to do so as well.

Life was going great in Los Angeles, until that night after a long day of photo shoot, when the commercial photographer invited Ron to celebrate the close of the shoot at a local bar with him. Several drinks later, Ron was in the man's bed, and, after sex, the man was whispering about having seen Ron on the Temptation Castle site the photographer used to peruse.

"You know the operation is still going," he murmured to Ron as they were lying in each other's arms, each fondling the other's dick.

"What do you mean?" Ron asked.

"After the original club burned down, the operation moved out here. A new Web site. Dream Ranch, it's called. The place is just an hour's drive south, at the base of the mountains. You should—"

"I don't think so," Ron answered, a bit more pointedly than he'd intended. "I've done with all that."

"You think so? You're here with me, aren't you?"

The photographer had dropped it at that, but the question plagued Ron all the way home in the hour before dawn when traffic was light enough for him to ruminate as he drove. The reason he'd been able to go with the photographer that night was that Sally and the girls were down in San Diego, visiting Susan and her boys. He was all alone in the house—for the entire weekend.

He'd had no intention of doing so, but it wasn't long after he'd gotten home that he found himself sitting at the computer, naked, and searching out the Dream Ranch Web site the photographer had spoken about, mentioning the URL. It had a similar code scheme to the Temptation Castle Web site. Ron had no trouble getting in—and getting down into the guts of the Web site far enough to confirm that both Matt and Theo were still alive—and as luscious, arousing, and tempting as ever.

~

About the Author

Habu is one of the pen names of a former supersonic spy jet pilot, intelligence agent, male model, movie actor, and diplomat. A wild youth in South East Asia was spent enjoying whatever sexual opportunities came his way, and much of his gay male writing is about recalling incidents from those days and inventing ones he'd perhaps have liked to experience. He now leads a very quiet and ordinary happily married family life.

An American, he is a published mainstream novelist and short story writer under another name and in another dimension of his life. He has written or cowritten (with Sabb) approaching 1,000 published short stories and over 100 published erotica e-books, primarily of gay fiction but also memoir, straight fiction and ménage fiction. His hand and creative writing can be seen in stories and books by habu, sr71plt, Dirk Hessian, Shabbu, and Stephen Kessel—among unrevealed others that might surprise readers. The fictionalized GM memoir *Flying High, Diving Deep* is loosely based on his life experiences. He can be found at the adults only gay male site www.BarbarianSpy.com, which he shares with Sabb and Dirk Hessian.

Our authors always like to receive feedback, and appreciate it when readers post reviews at distributors and other sites.

FOR LITERARY HEAT

Not all books listed below may currently be on release.
* indicates the book is available in paperback and e-book.

BOOKS BY CHRIS CROSS
Multisexual Adult Romance
Pulaski Square

BOOKS BY ALEX LOCKHEED
Transgender Romance
Meeting Jenna
Transgender Other
Being Sarah

BOOKS BY DIRK HESSIAN
Xtreme Historical Erotica
The King's Men
Shores of Tripoli
Prophecy of Noto
Pretender's Fate
General Historical Erotic Romance
To the Hessian Hills
Fire Down the Valley*
Constantinople*
The Beautiful Way*
Blue and Gray
Colonel's Treasure
Beginning of Time
Labyrinth

BOOKS BY HABU
Gay Erotica
Memoir Faction
Flying High, Diving Deep*
Xtreme Erotica
Tramp Steaming*
Escape to Girne
Silas' Choice*
Last Call
Choke Hold
Apyko: The Greek Pimp
Visits of the Schlange
Second Coming: Emile La Cour Unleashed
Vortex: Sacrificed by Curiosity*
Dark Angel Sounding *(in e-book & included in Sounding:Ultimate Control Paperback)**
Sounding: Ultimate Control *(Print Only)**
Sounding Five *(in e-book & included in Sounding:Ultimate Control paperback)**
Romance
Rain Check
Built for Pleasure (Sci Fi)
Danny's Choice
Pull of the Groove
Sugar n Spice Christmas
Friday Nights with Lenny (Christmas Romance)
Snowy, Snowy Nights (Christmas Romance)
Tank n Bull
Sail to the Sun
War Letters
Ravens Roost
Caribbean Cruise Top to Bottom
Arena Stage
Trading Partners (Valentine's Day)
Four Coins
Lower Than the Heart (Valentine's Day)
Brambleton
Gotta Keep Trying

Finding Amnad
Platres Conclave
Other Novels/Novellas
Temptation's Clutches*
Descent into Chaos
Escape to Girne
Journey Through Abilene
Harmony and Dissonance
Stallion Station
Racing With the Devil (espionage suspense)
Cruising Gigolo (bisexual)
Prepared in Cape Verdi
Gilded Cage
House on Park*
Anything for Ambition
Dance of the Ravishers
Hard Knocks U*
My Neighbor's Spa*
Man's Man: Tales of a High Priced Gay Hooker*
Trip Money
The Indian Doctor
Sailorboy
Home to Fire Island
Murder Mysteries
Death on a Ping Pong Table
Clint Folsom Mysteries Compendium Volume 1*
Death to Blonds - Stolen Judgment (Clint Folsom Mystery)*
Clint Folsom Mysteries Compendium Volume 2*
Gay Erotica Anthologies
Earth Cry*
Shunga
Habu's Christmas Balls
Eight in D*
DevilMENt
Silas' Choices*
Stallion Station (A Novella in Parts)
Eleven to the Dogs*
Fifty Seventy*

Spy Tails 001*
Spy Tails 002*
Doubled*
Doubled Again*
Tails in the Tropics*
Tails in the Med*
Tails in the West*
Rough Riders*
Grab Bag 1*
Grab Bag 2*
Grab Bag 3*
Grab Bag 4*
Grab Bag 5*
Grab Bag 6*
Grab Bag 7*
Beyond the Beaded Curtain*
Habu's Christmas Balls
The Sporting Life*
Fetish Galore!*
Literary Gay Erotica
Cairo Surrender*
The Handyman*
Homeward Bound
Journey to Mirage*
Bi-Sexual/Menage Erotica
Bisexual/Menage/Multisexual Erotica
Two Men, One Woman*
Every Which Way
Vanishing Laura
Summer of Denial
Death on a Ping Pong Table
Cruising Gigolo
13 Ways for Halloween
Luther*
The Indian Prince*
MF Erotica
Chocolate in Vanilla*
BOOKS BY SABB

Driver Reliever
Hiring in Hollywood
The Legend of Holleystone Grange
Surprise Encounters*
She is He
Wrong Man
Loyal to his King
Barbarian Tales - Book One - Traveler's Tales*
Barbarian Tales - Book Two - Journeys Begin*
Barbarian Tales - Book Three - The Inheritance*
Barbarian Tales - Book Four - Road to Persepolis*

BOOKS BY SHABBU
Velvet Interrogation
Finding Jason
Dirty Pool
Operation Black Jade
Cigars!*
Angel in the Barn
Gayly Complicated*
Despoiling David
The Tree of Idleness*
I Met a Man
Rough Road to Happiness

BOOKS BY STEPHEN KESSEL
Gay Romance
The Forever Man
Two Chances

BOOKS BY KIM BLACK
Lesbian Romance
Transfixed on Tammie (F/T lesbian)